THOU SHALT NOT...

Kris Oprisko
Renato Guedes
Ashley Wood

IDW Publishing
San Diego, California

CSI: Miami™
Created by **Anthony E. Zuiker**

Licensed to IDW by CBS Consumer Products

Thou Shalt Not...

Written by **Kris Oprisko**

Art by **Renato Guedes**

Painted Artwork by **Ashley Wood**

Lettered by **Robbie Robbins**

Edited by **Jeff Mariotte**

Cover photo by **Blake Edwards**

Book Design by **Cindy Chapman**

Special thanks to Maryann Martin and Ken Ross at CBS Consumer Products for their invaluable assistance.

ISBN: 1-932382-25-9
07 06 05 04   1 2 3 4 5

www.IDWPUBLISHING.COM

IDW Publishing is:
Ted Adams, Publisher
Jeff Mariotte, Editor-in-Chief
Robbie Robbins, Design Director
Kris Oprisko, Vice President
Alex Garner, Art Director
Cindy Chapman, Design
Beau Smith, Sales and Marketing
Lorelei Bunjes, Media Coordinator
Brian Berling, Editorial Assistant
Chance Boren, Editorial Assistant
Yumiko Miyano, Business Development
Rick Privman, Business Development

CSI: MIAMI—THOU SHALT NOT.... April 2004. FIRST PRINTING. IDW Publishing, a division of Idea + Design Works, LLC. Editorial Offices: 4411 Morena Blvd., Suite 106, San Diego, CA 92117. CSI: Miami © 2004 CBS Broadcasting Inc. and Alliance Atlantis Productions, Inc. CBS Broadcasting Inc. and Alliance Atlantis Productions, Inc. are the authors of this program for the purposes of copyright and other laws. ™ CBS Broadcasting Inc. All Rights Reserved. © 2004 Idea + Design Works, LLC. All Rights Reserved. Any similarities to persons living or dead are purely coincidental. With the exception of artwork used for review purposes, none of the contents of this publication may be reprinted without the permission of Idea + Design Works, LLC. Printed in Republic of Korea.

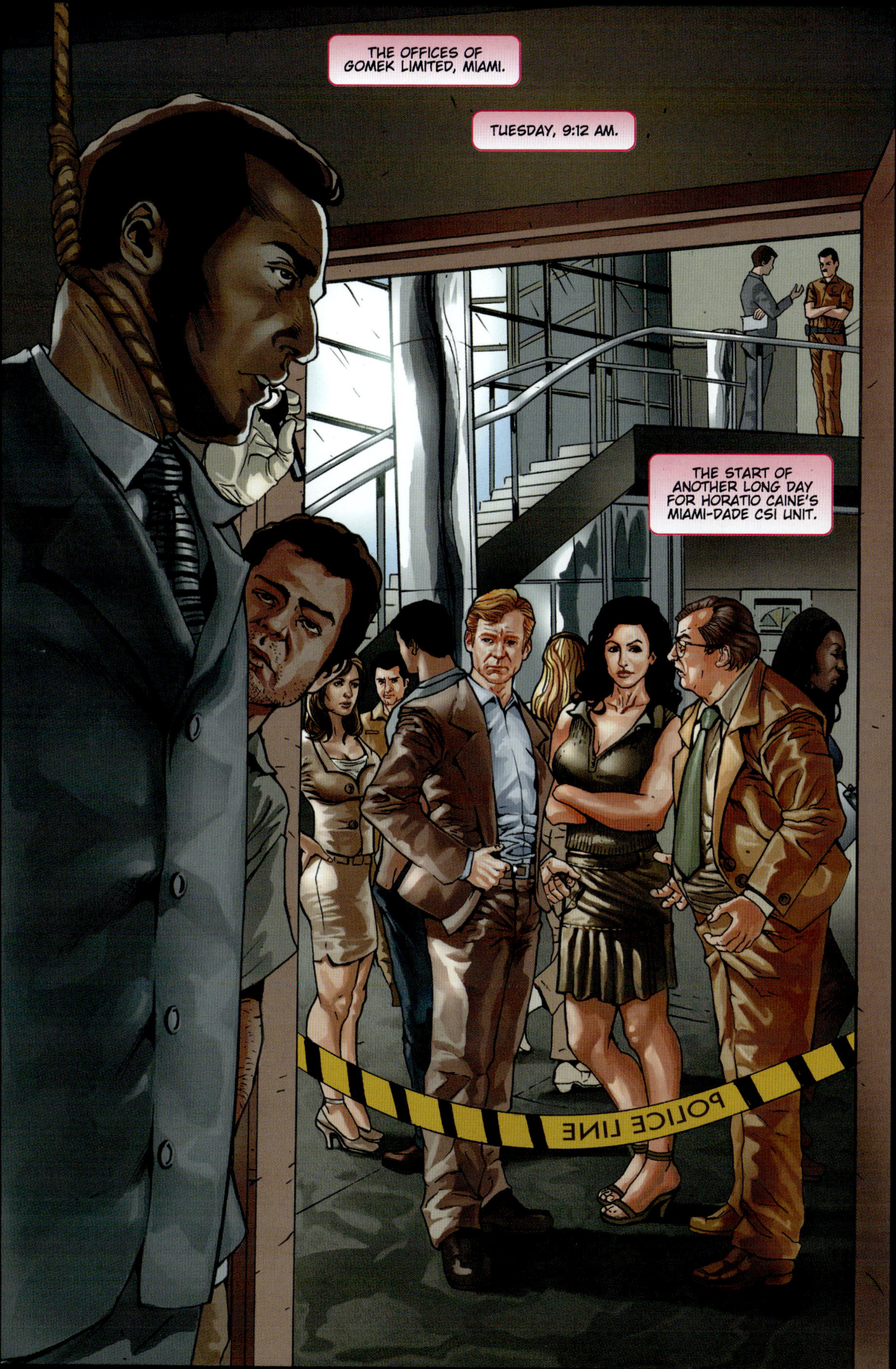
THE OFFICES OF GOMEK LIMITED, MIAMI.
TUESDAY, 9:12 AM.
THE START OF ANOTHER LONG DAY FOR HORATIO CAINE'S MIAMI-DADE CSI UNIT.
POLICE LINE

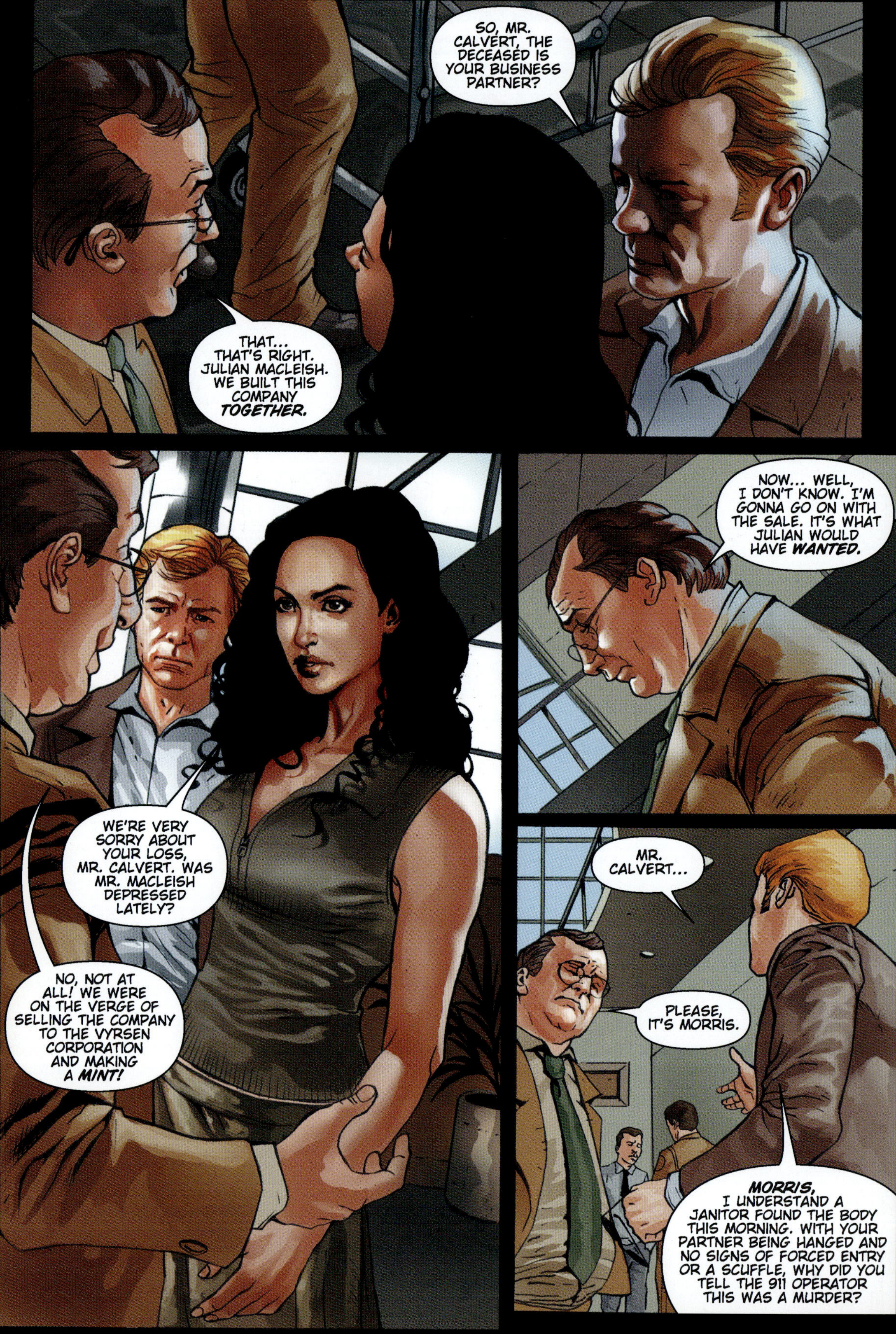

SO, MR. CALVERT, THE DECEASED IS YOUR BUSINESS PARTNER?
THAT... THAT'S RIGHT. JULIAN MACLEISH. WE BUILT THIS COMPANY *TOGETHER.*
WE'RE VERY SORRY ABOUT YOUR LOSS, MR. CALVERT. WAS MR. MACLEISH DEPRESSED LATELY?
NO, NOT AT ALL! WE WERE ON THE VERGE OF SELLING THE COMPANY TO THE VYRSEN CORPORATION AND MAKING A *MINT!*
NOW... WELL, I DON'T KNOW. I'M GONNA GO ON WITH THE SALE. IT'S WHAT JULIAN WOULD HAVE *WANTED.*
MR. CALVERT...
PLEASE, IT'S MORRIS.
MORRIS, I UNDERSTAND A JANITOR FOUND THE BODY THIS MORNING. WITH YOUR PARTNER BEING HANGED AND NO SIGNS OF FORCED ENTRY OR A SCUFFLE, WHY DID YOU TELL THE 911 OPERATOR THIS WAS A MURDER?

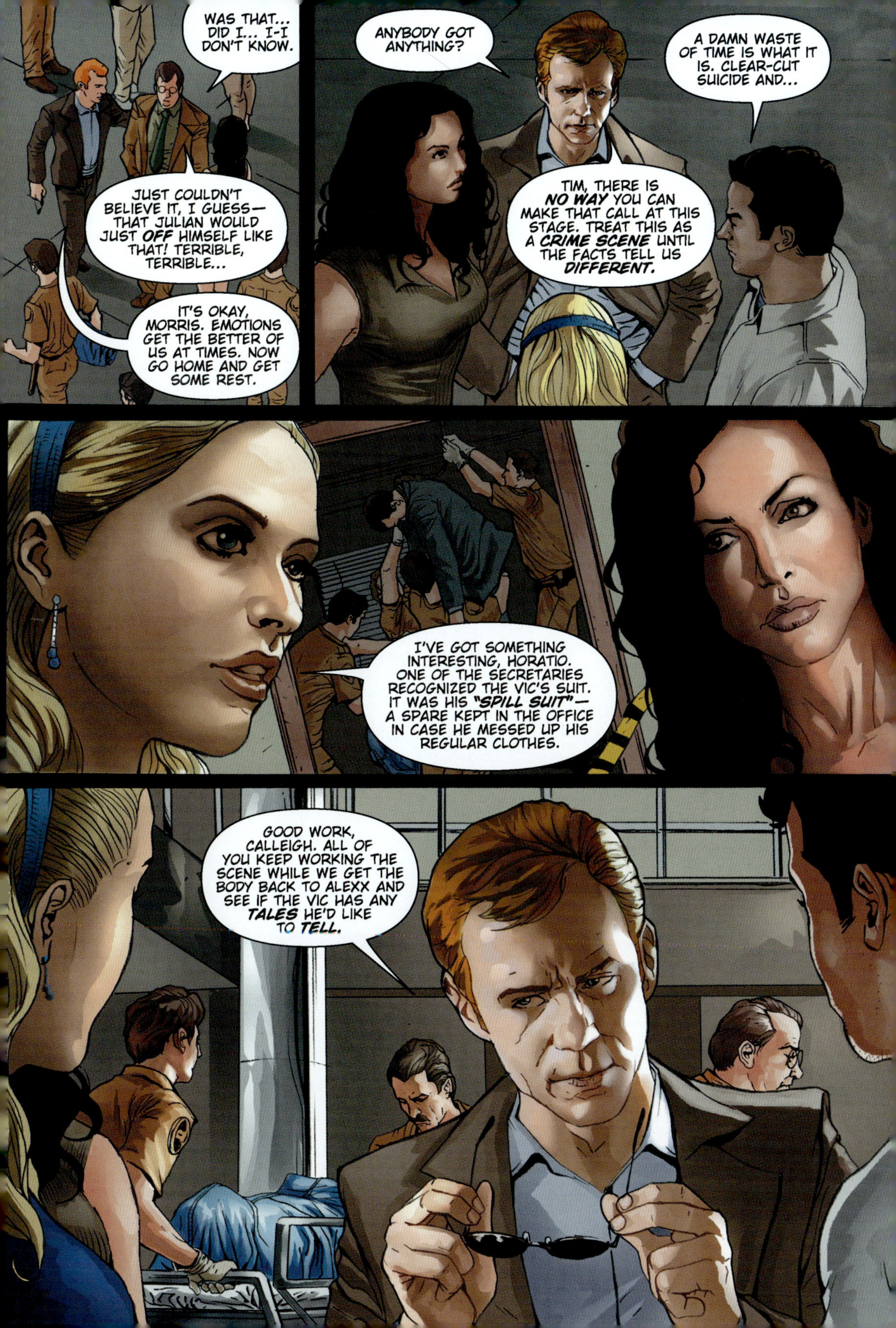
WAS THAT... DID I... I-I DON'T KNOW.
JUST COULDN'T BELIEVE IT, I GUESS— THAT JULIAN WOULD JUST OFF HIMSELF LIKE THAT! TERRIBLE, TERRIBLE...
IT'S OKAY, MORRIS. EMOTIONS GET THE BETTER OF US AT TIMES. NOW GO HOME AND GET SOME REST.
ANYBODY GOT ANYTHING?
A DAMN WASTE OF TIME IS WHAT IT IS. CLEAR-CUT SUICIDE AND...
TIM, THERE IS NO WAY YOU CAN MAKE THAT CALL AT THIS STAGE. TREAT THIS AS A CRIME SCENE UNTIL THE FACTS TELL US DIFFERENT.
I'VE GOT SOMETHING INTERESTING, HORATIO. ONE OF THE SECRETARIES RECOGNIZED THE VIC'S SUIT. IT WAS HIS "SPILL SUIT"— A SPARE KEPT IN THE OFFICE IN CASE HE MESSED UP HIS REGULAR CLOTHES.
GOOD WORK, CALLEIGH. ALL OF YOU KEEP WORKING THE SCENE WHILE WE GET THE BODY BACK TO ALEXX AND SEE IF THE VIC HAS ANY TALES HE'D LIKE TO TELL.

LATER, CSI CRIME LAB.

"...SO I PLACE THE TIME OF DEATH SOMETIME ON MONDAY EVENING. BUT THAT'S NOT THE MOST *INTERESTING* THING I'VE FOUND."

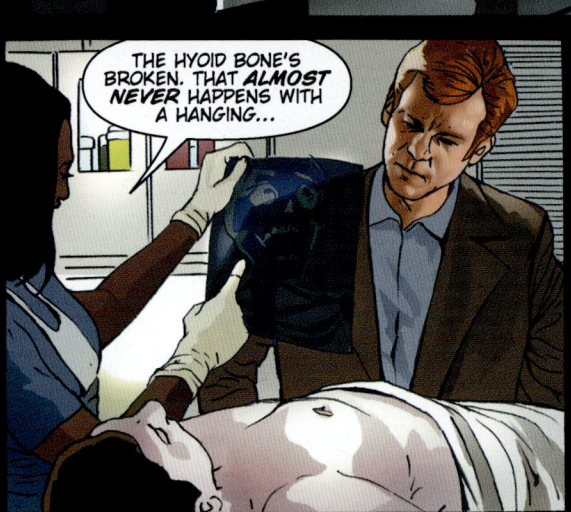

"THE HYOID BONE'S BROKEN. THAT *ALMOST NEVER* HAPPENS WITH A HANGING..."

"...BUT IT'S COMMON WITH STRANGULATION."

"TRUE, BUT IT'S STILL *POSSIBLE*. WE CAN'T JUMP TO CONCLUSIONS WITHOUT MORE *FACTS*. GOT ANYTHING ELSE?"

"OH, YES, HORATIO..."

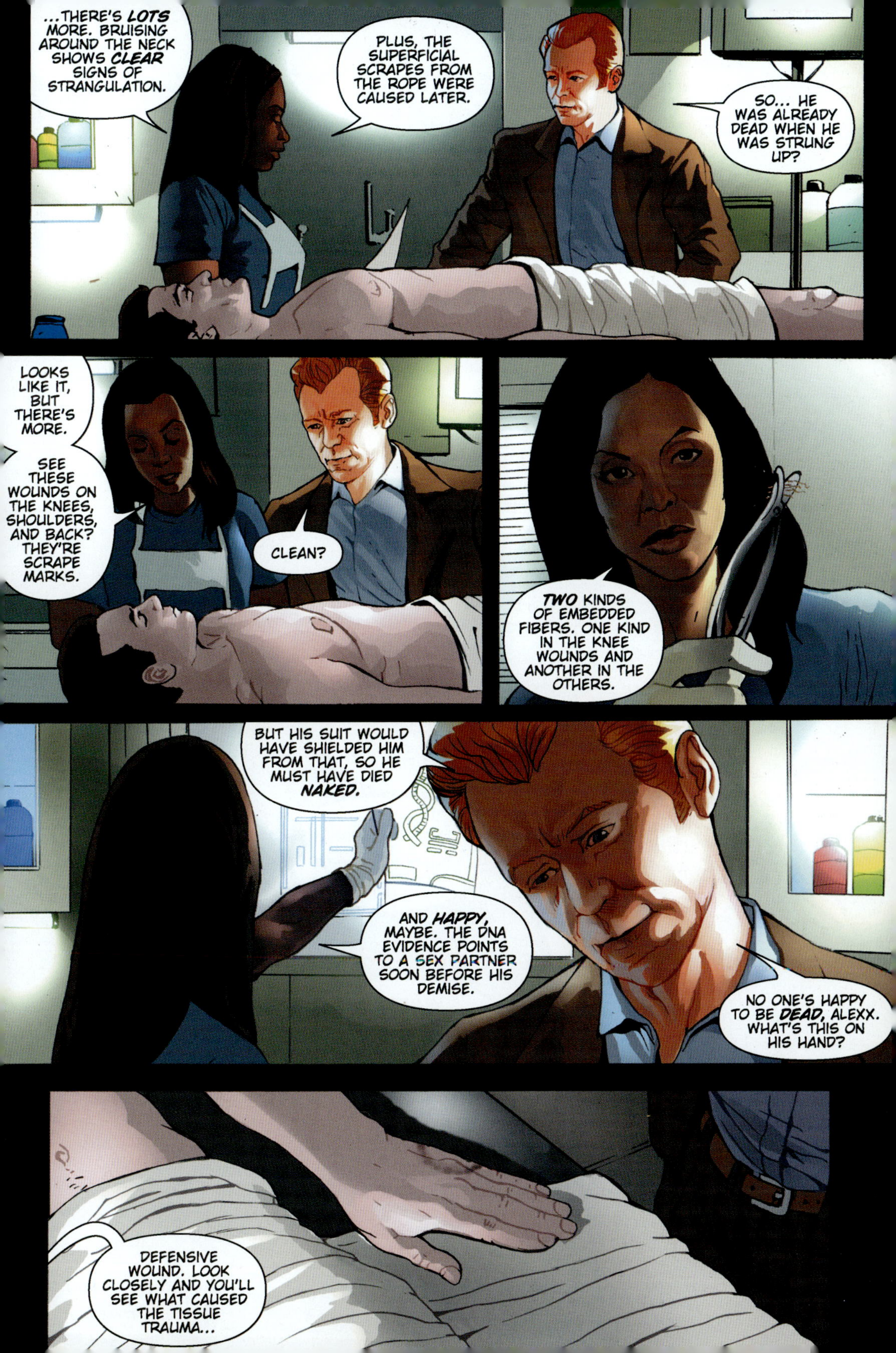
...THERE'S LOTS MORE. BRUISING AROUND THE NECK SHOWS CLEAR SIGNS OF STRANGULATION.
PLUS, THE SUPERFICIAL SCRAPES FROM THE ROPE WERE CAUSED LATER.
SO... HE WAS ALREADY DEAD WHEN HE WAS STRUNG UP?
LOOKS LIKE IT, BUT THERE'S MORE.
SEE THESE WOUNDS ON THE KNEES, SHOULDERS, AND BACK? THEY'RE SCRAPE MARKS.
CLEAN?
TWO KINDS OF EMBEDDED FIBERS. ONE KIND IN THE KNEE WOUNDS AND ANOTHER IN THE OTHERS.
BUT HIS SUIT WOULD HAVE SHIELDED HIM FROM THAT, SO HE MUST HAVE DIED NAKED.
AND HAPPY, MAYBE. THE DNA EVIDENCE POINTS TO A SEX PARTNER SOON BEFORE HIS DEMISE.
NO ONE'S HAPPY TO BE DEAD, ALEXX. WHAT'S THIS ON HIS HAND?
DEFENSIVE WOUND. LOOK CLOSELY AND YOU'LL SEE WHAT CAUSED THE TISSUE TRAUMA...

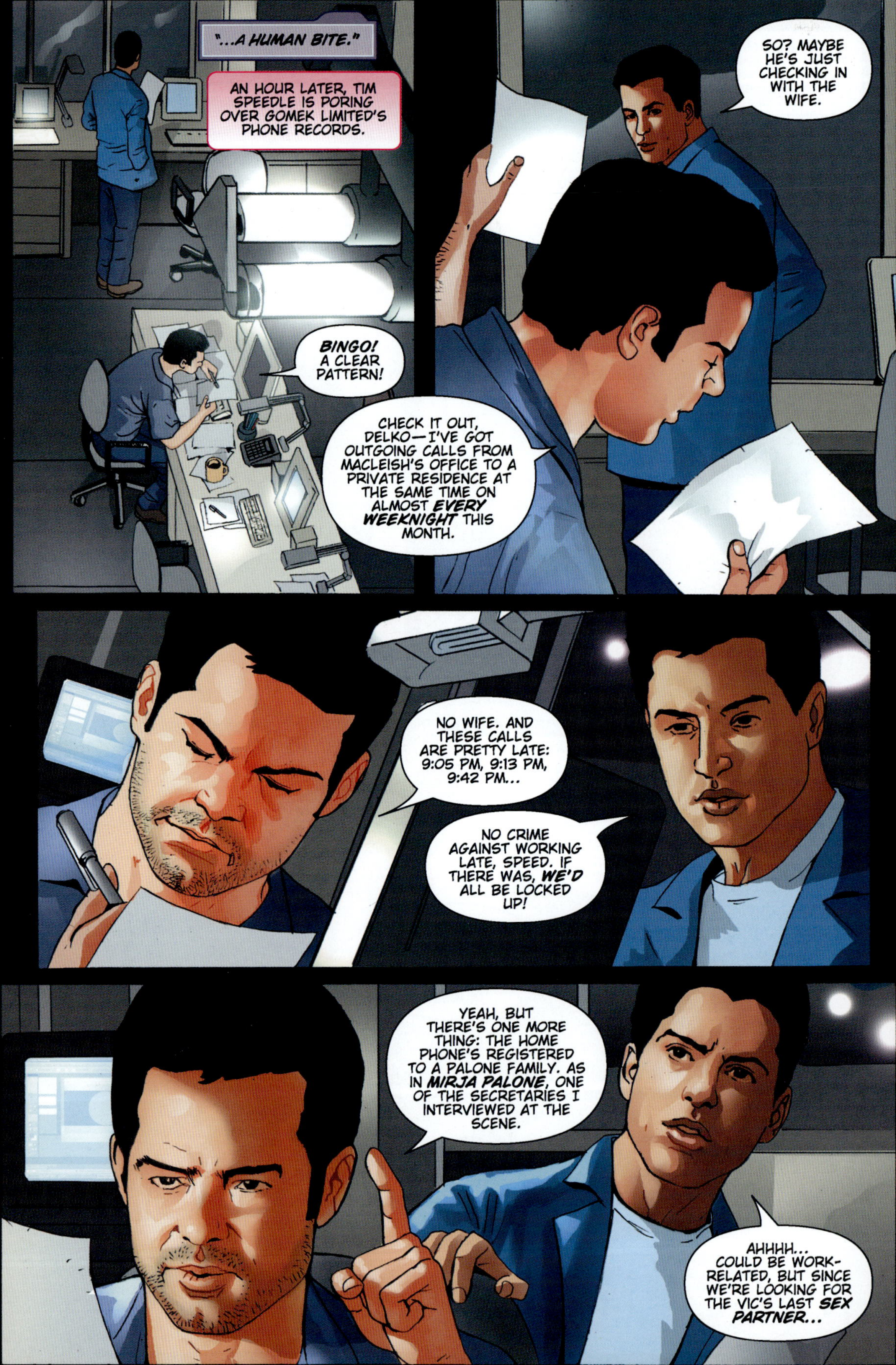
"...A HUMAN BITE."
AN HOUR LATER, TIM SPEEDLE IS PORING OVER GOMEK LIMITED'S PHONE RECORDS.
BINGO! A CLEAR PATTERN!
CHECK IT OUT, DELKO—I'VE GOT OUTGOING CALLS FROM MACLEISH'S OFFICE TO A PRIVATE RESIDENCE AT THE SAME TIME ON ALMOST EVERY WEEKNIGHT THIS MONTH.
SO? MAYBE HE'S JUST CHECKING IN WITH THE WIFE.
NO WIFE. AND THESE CALLS ARE PRETTY LATE: 9:05 PM, 9:13 PM, 9:42 PM...
NO CRIME AGAINST WORKING LATE, SPEED. IF THERE WAS, WE'D ALL BE LOCKED UP!
YEAH, BUT THERE'S ONE MORE THING: THE HOME PHONE'S REGISTERED TO A PALONE FAMILY. AS IN MIRJA PALONE, ONE OF THE SECRETARIES I INTERVIEWED AT THE SCENE.
AHHHH... COULD BE WORK-RELATED, BUT SINCE WE'RE LOOKING FOR THE VIC'S LAST SEX PARTNER...

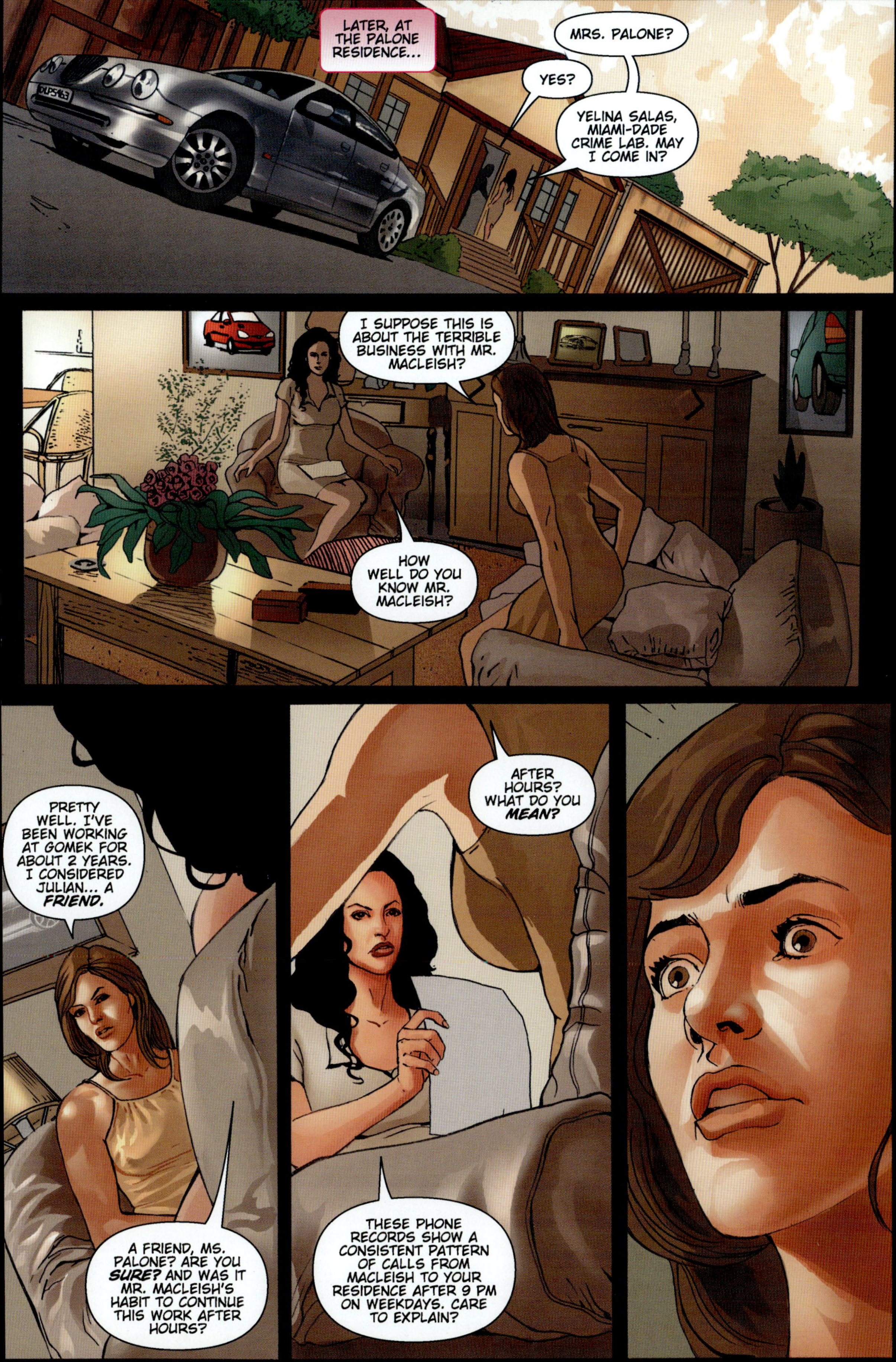
LATER, AT THE PALONE RESIDENCE...
MRS. PALONE?
YES?
YELINA SALAS, MIAMI-DADE CRIME LAB. MAY I COME IN?
I SUPPOSE THIS IS ABOUT THE TERRIBLE BUSINESS WITH MR. MACLEISH?
HOW WELL DO YOU KNOW MR. MACLEISH?
PRETTY WELL. I'VE BEEN WORKING AT GOMEK FOR ABOUT 2 YEARS. I CONSIDERED JULIAN... A *FRIEND.*
A FRIEND, MS. PALONE? ARE YOU *SURE?* AND WAS IT MR. MACLEISH'S HABIT TO CONTINUE THIS WORK AFTER HOURS?
AFTER HOURS? WHAT DO YOU *MEAN?*
THESE PHONE RECORDS SHOW A CONSISTENT PATTERN OF CALLS FROM MACLEISH TO YOUR RESIDENCE AFTER 9 PM ON WEEKDAYS. CARE TO EXPLAIN?

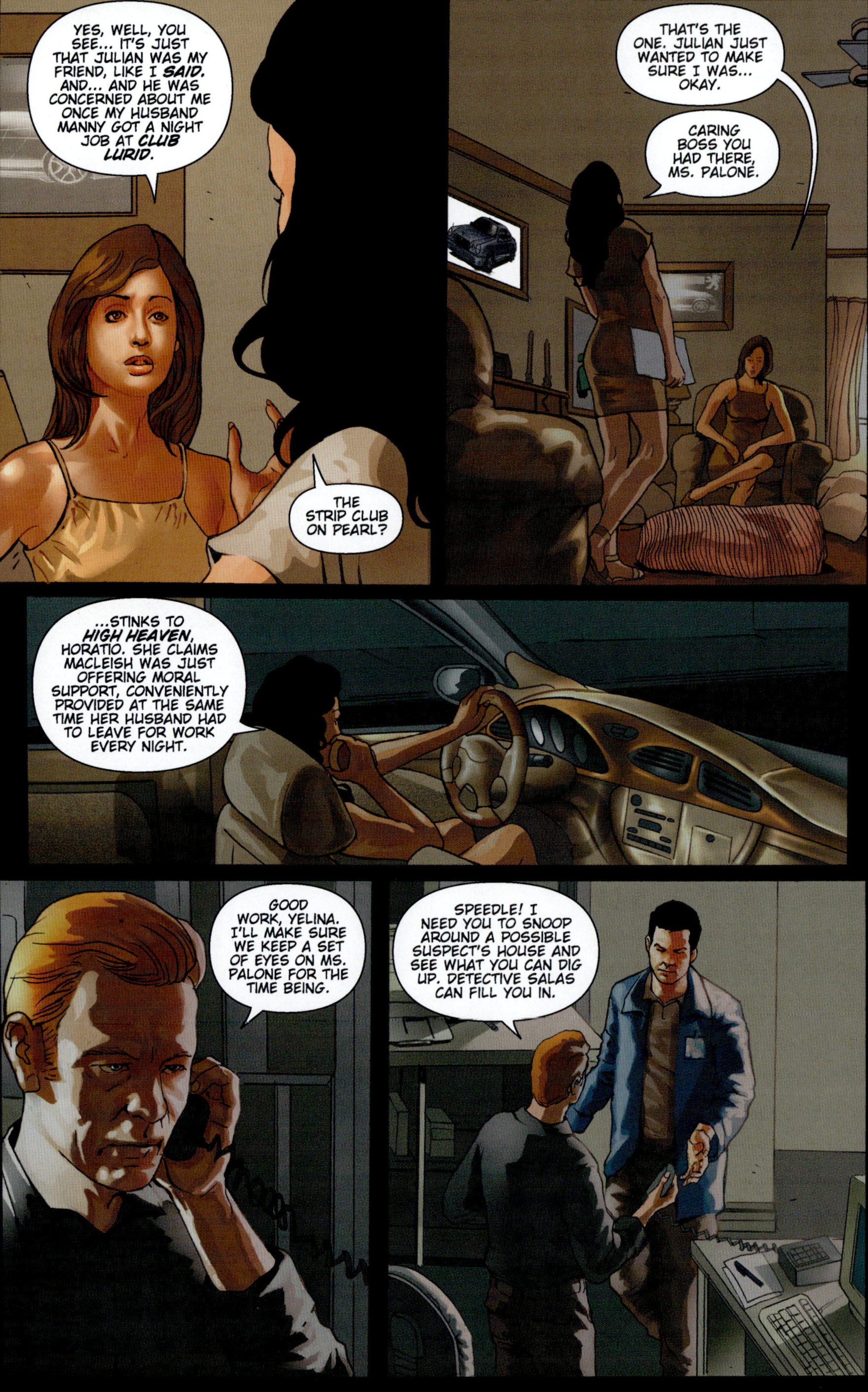

YES, WELL, YOU SEE... IT'S JUST THAT JULIAN WAS MY FRIEND, LIKE I *SAID.* AND... AND HE WAS CONCERNED ABOUT ME ONCE MY HUSBAND MANNY GOT A NIGHT JOB AT ***CLUB LURID.***
THE STRIP CLUB ON PEARL?
THAT'S THE ONE. JULIAN JUST WANTED TO MAKE SURE I WAS... OKAY.
CARING BOSS YOU HAD THERE, MS. PALONE.
...STINKS TO ***HIGH HEAVEN***, HORATIO. SHE CLAIMS MACLEISH WAS JUST OFFERING MORAL SUPPORT, CONVENIENTLY PROVIDED AT THE SAME TIME HER HUSBAND HAD TO LEAVE FOR WORK EVERY NIGHT.
GOOD WORK, YELINA. I'LL MAKE SURE WE KEEP A SET OF EYES ON MS. PALONE FOR THE TIME BEING.
SPEEDLE! I NEED YOU TO SNOOP AROUND A POSSIBLE SUSPECT'S HOUSE AND SEE WHAT YOU CAN DIG UP. DETECTIVE SALAS CAN FILL YOU IN.

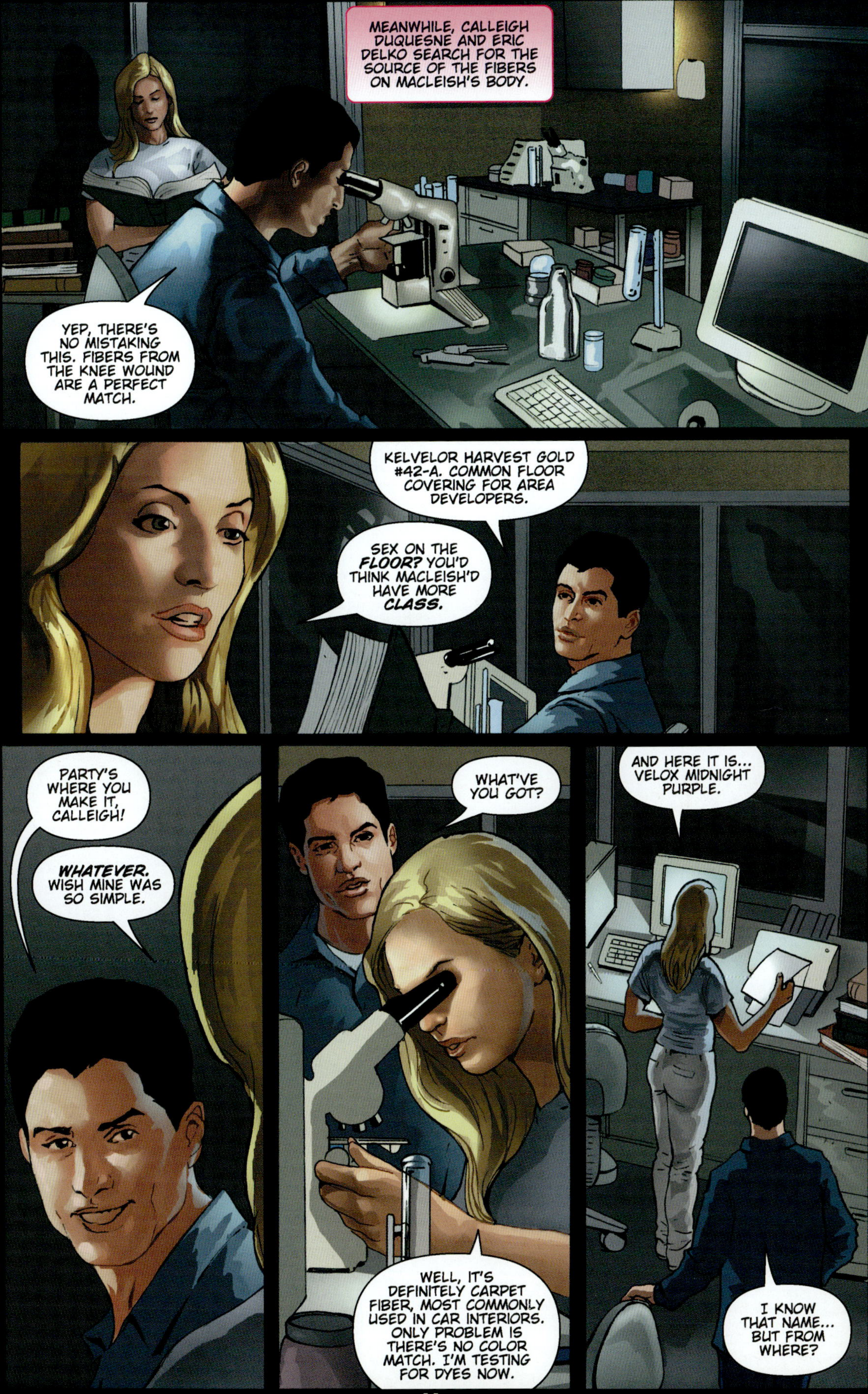
MEANWHILE, CALLEIGH DUQUESNE AND ERIC DELKO SEARCH FOR THE SOURCE OF THE FIBERS ON MACLEISH'S BODY.
YEP, THERE'S NO MISTAKING THIS. FIBERS FROM THE KNEE WOUND ARE A PERFECT MATCH.
KELVELOR HARVEST GOLD #42-A. COMMON FLOOR COVERING FOR AREA DEVELOPERS.
SEX ON THE FLOOR? YOU'D THINK MACLEISH'D HAVE MORE CLASS.
PARTY'S WHERE YOU MAKE IT, CALLEIGH!
WHATEVER. WISH MINE WAS SO SIMPLE.
WHAT'VE YOU GOT?
WELL, IT'S DEFINITELY CARPET FIBER, MOST COMMONLY USED IN CAR INTERIORS. ONLY PROBLEM IS THERE'S NO COLOR MATCH. I'M TESTING FOR DYES NOW.
AND HERE IT IS... VELOX MIDNIGHT PURPLE.
I KNOW THAT NAME... BUT FROM WHERE?

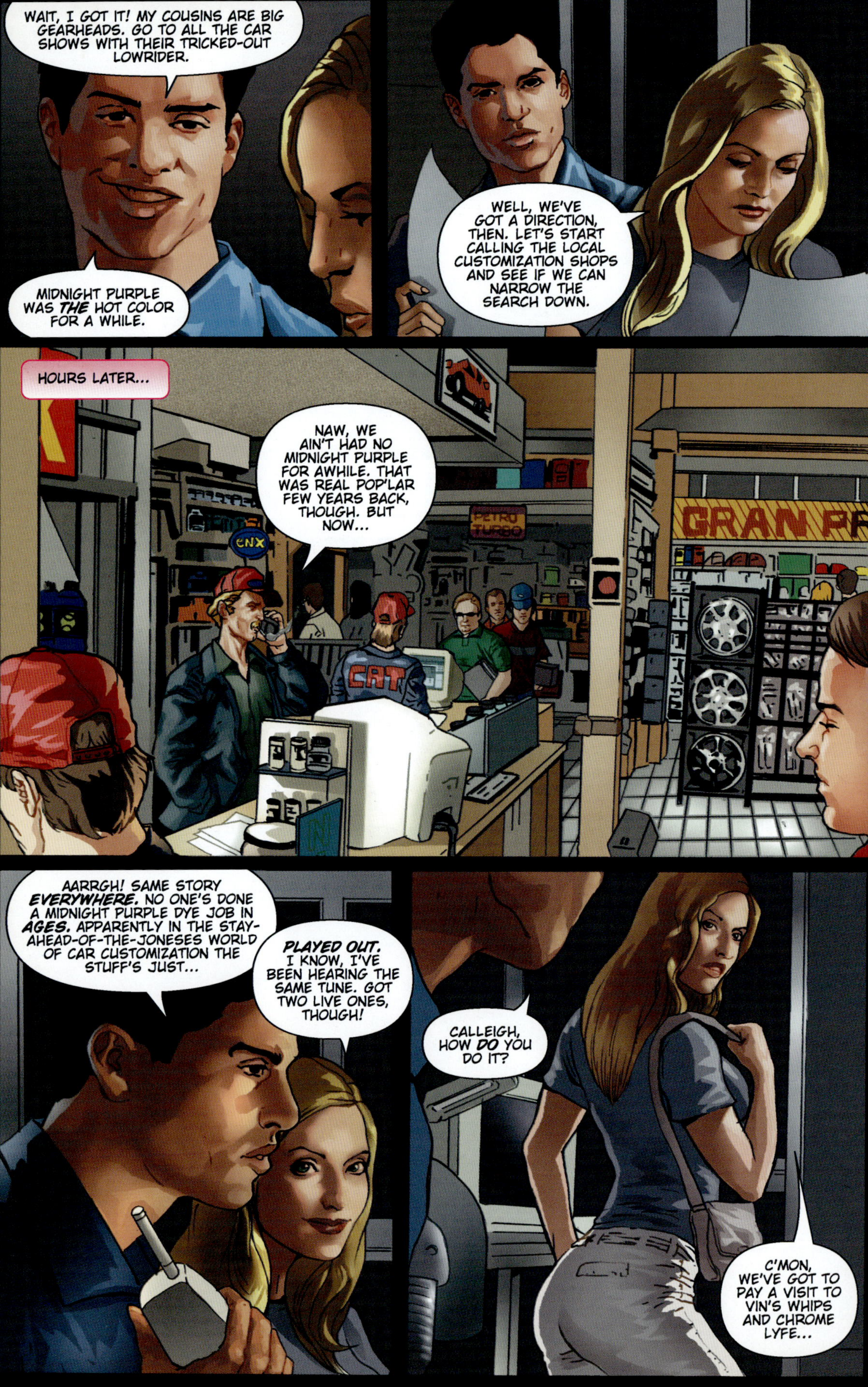

WAIT, I GOT IT! MY COUSINS ARE BIG GEARHEADS. GO TO ALL THE CAR SHOWS WITH THEIR TRICKED-OUT LOWRIDER.
MIDNIGHT PURPLE WAS *THE* HOT COLOR FOR A WHILE.
WELL, WE'VE GOT A DIRECTION, THEN. LET'S START CALLING THE LOCAL CUSTOMIZATION SHOPS AND SEE IF WE CAN NARROW THE SEARCH DOWN.
HOURS LATER...
NAW, WE AIN'T HAD NO MIDNIGHT PURPLE FOR AWHILE. THAT WAS REAL POP'LAR FEW YEARS BACK, THOUGH. BUT NOW...
CNX
PETRO TURBO
GRAN P
CAT
AARRGH! SAME STORY *EVERYWHERE.* NO ONE'S DONE A MIDNIGHT PURPLE DYE JOB IN *AGES.* APPARENTLY IN THE STAY-AHEAD-OF-THE-JONESES WORLD OF CAR CUSTOMIZATION THE STUFF'S JUST...
PLAYED OUT. I KNOW, I'VE BEEN HEARING THE SAME TUNE. GOT TWO LIVE ONES, THOUGH!
CALLEIGH, HOW *DO* YOU DO IT?
C'MON, WE'VE GOT TO PAY A VISIT TO VIN'S WHIPS AND CHROME LYFE...

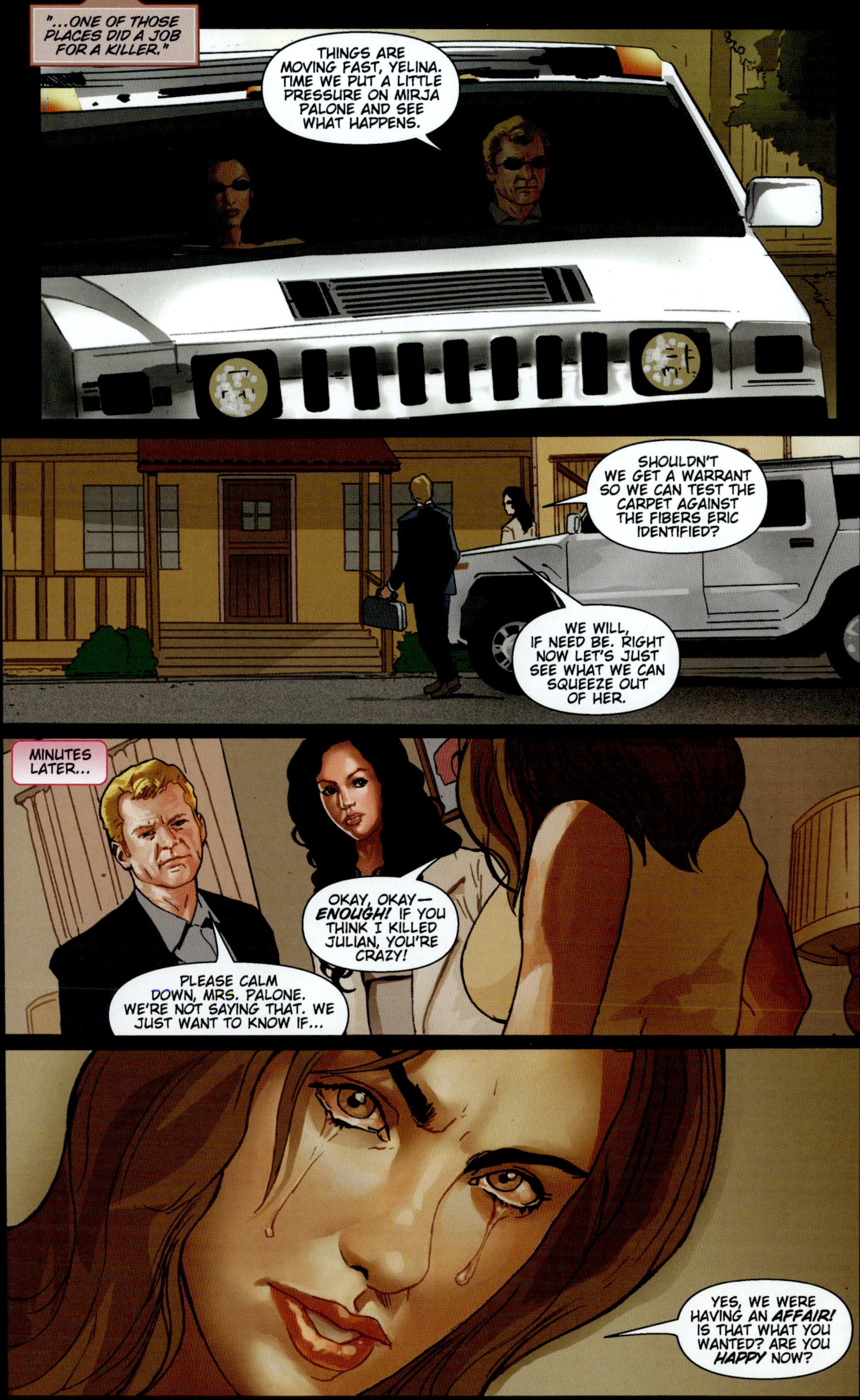
"...ONE OF THOSE PLACES DID A JOB FOR A KILLER."
THINGS ARE MOVING FAST, YELINA. TIME WE PUT A LITTLE PRESSURE ON MIRJA PALONE AND SEE WHAT HAPPENS.
SHOULDN'T WE GET A WARRANT SO WE CAN TEST THE CARPET AGAINST THE FIBERS ERIC IDENTIFIED?
WE WILL, IF NEED BE. RIGHT NOW LET'S JUST SEE WHAT WE CAN SQUEEZE OUT OF HER.
MINUTES LATER...
OKAY, OKAY— ENOUGH! IF YOU THINK I KILLED JULIAN, YOU'RE CRAZY!
PLEASE CALM DOWN, MRS. PALONE. WE'RE NOT SAYING THAT. WE JUST WANT TO KNOW IF...
YES, WE WERE HAVING AN AFFAIR! IS THAT WHAT YOU WANTED? ARE YOU HAPPY NOW?

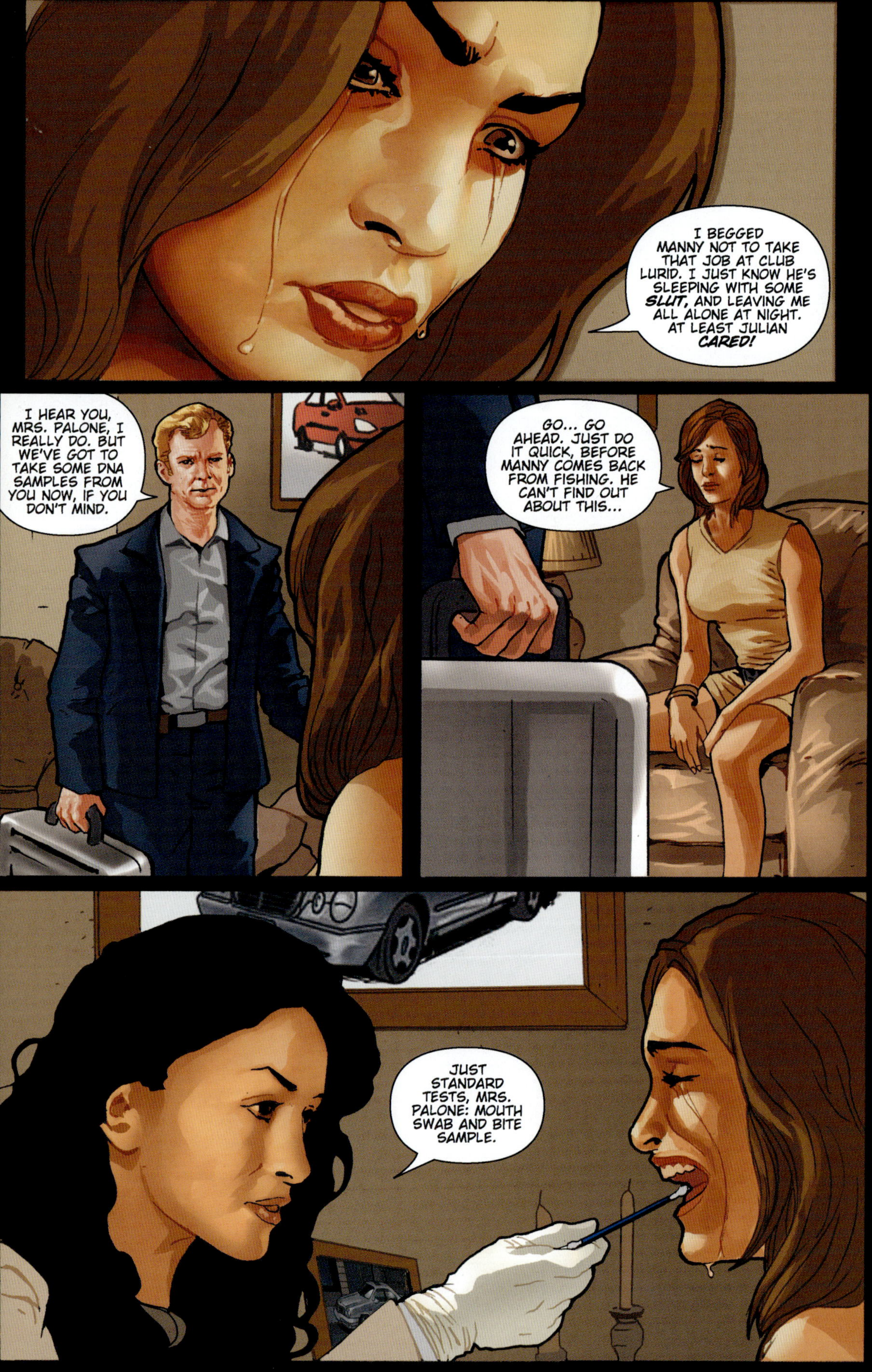
I BEGGED MANNY NOT TO TAKE THAT JOB AT CLUB LURID. I JUST KNOW HE'S SLEEPING WITH SOME *SLUT*, AND LEAVING ME ALL ALONE AT NIGHT. AT LEAST JULIAN *CARED!*
I HEAR YOU, MRS. PALONE, I REALLY DO. BUT WE'VE GOT TO TAKE SOME DNA SAMPLES FROM YOU NOW, IF YOU DON'T MIND.
GO... GO AHEAD. JUST DO IT QUICK, BEFORE MANNY COMES BACK FROM FISHING. HE CAN'T FIND OUT ABOUT THIS...
JUST STANDARD TESTS, MRS. PALONE: MOUTH SWAB AND BITE SAMPLE.

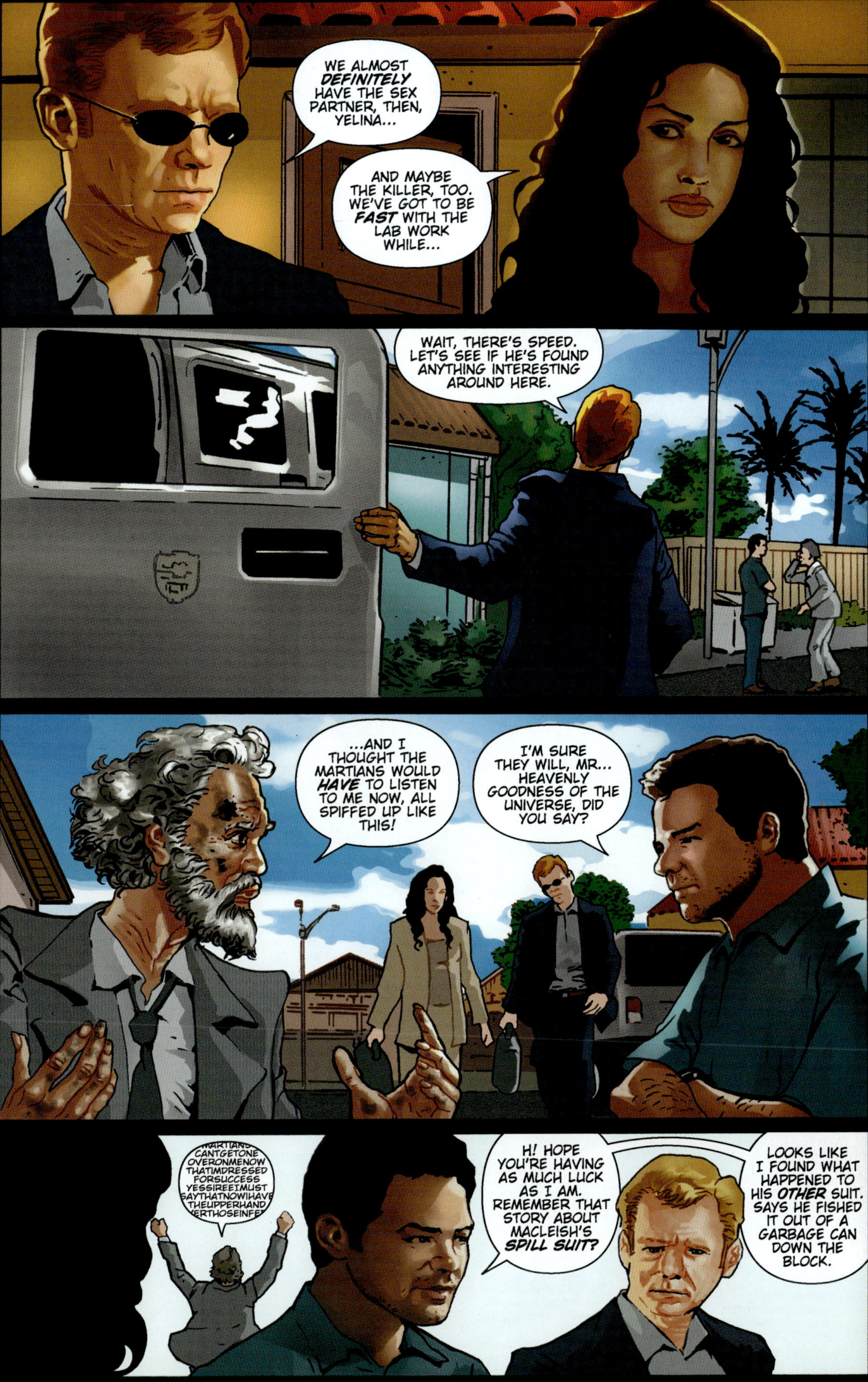
WE ALMOST DEFINITELY HAVE THE SEX PARTNER, THEN, YELINA...
AND MAYBE THE KILLER, TOO. WE'VE GOT TO BE FAST WITH THE LAB WORK WHILE...
WAIT, THERE'S SPEED. LET'S SEE IF HE'S FOUND ANYTHING INTERESTING AROUND HERE.
...AND I THOUGHT THE MARTIANS WOULD HAVE TO LISTEN TO ME NOW, ALL SPIFFED UP LIKE THIS!
I'M SURE THEY WILL, MR... HEAVENLY GOODNESS OF THE UNIVERSE, DID YOU SAY?
CANTGETONE OVERONMENOW THATIMDRESSED FORSUCCESS YESSIREEIMUST SAYTHATNOWIHAVE THEUPPERHAND
H! HOPE YOU'RE HAVING AS MUCH LUCK AS I AM. REMEMBER THAT STORY ABOUT MACLEISH'S SPILL SUIT?
LOOKS LIKE I FOUND WHAT HAPPENED TO HIS OTHER SUIT. SAYS HE FISHED IT OUT OF A GARBAGE CAN DOWN THE BLOCK.

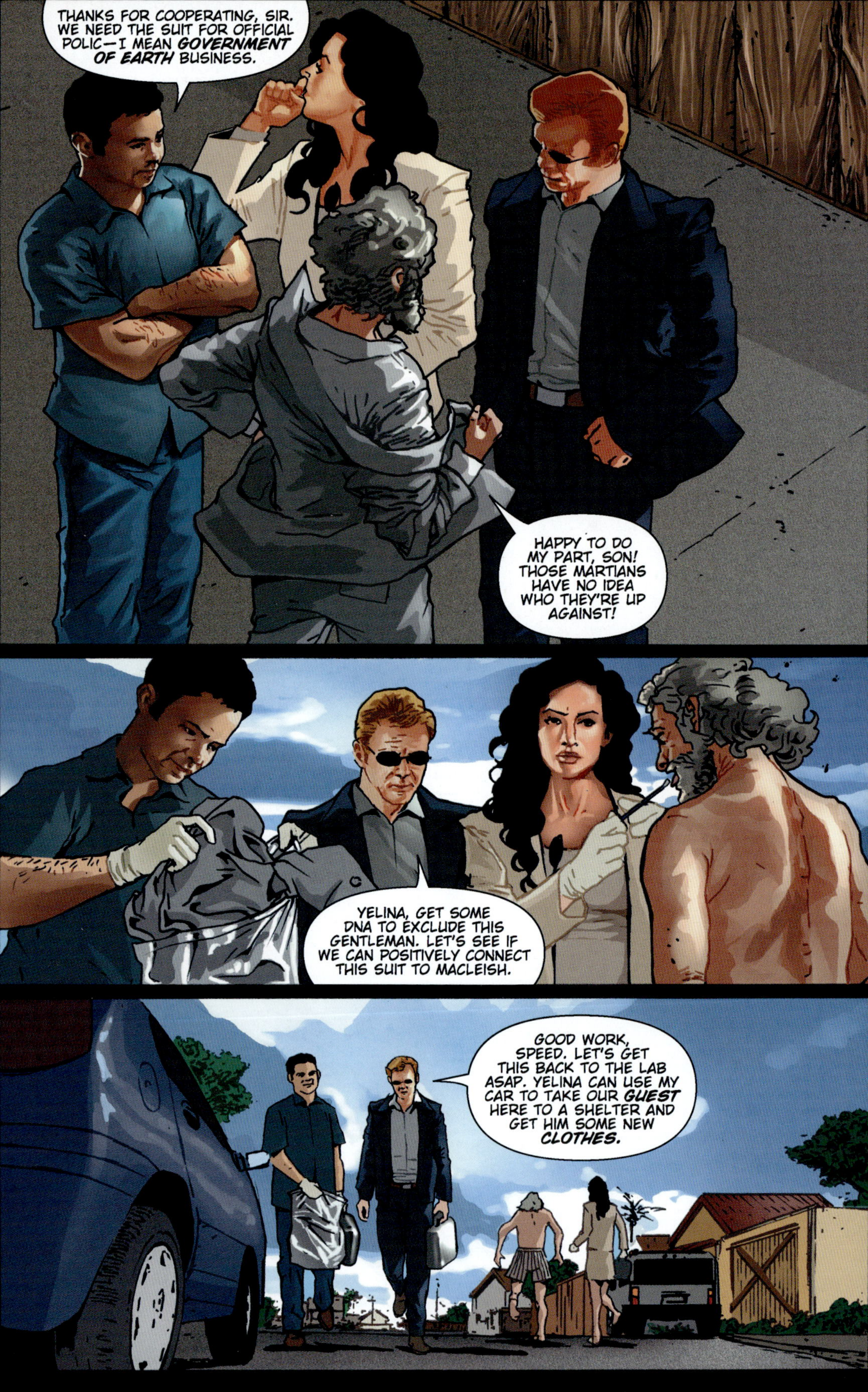
THANKS FOR COOPERATING, SIR. WE NEED THE SUIT FOR OFFICIAL POLIC—I MEAN GOVERNMENT OF EARTH BUSINESS.
HAPPY TO DO MY PART, SON! THOSE MARTIANS HAVE NO IDEA WHO THEY'RE UP AGAINST!
YELINA, GET SOME DNA TO EXCLUDE THIS GENTLEMAN. LET'S SEE IF WE CAN POSITIVELY CONNECT THIS SUIT TO MACLEISH.
GOOD WORK, SPEED. LET'S GET THIS BACK TO THE LAB ASAP. YELINA CAN USE MY CAR TO TAKE OUR GUEST HERE TO A SHELTER AND GET HIM SOME NEW CLOTHES.

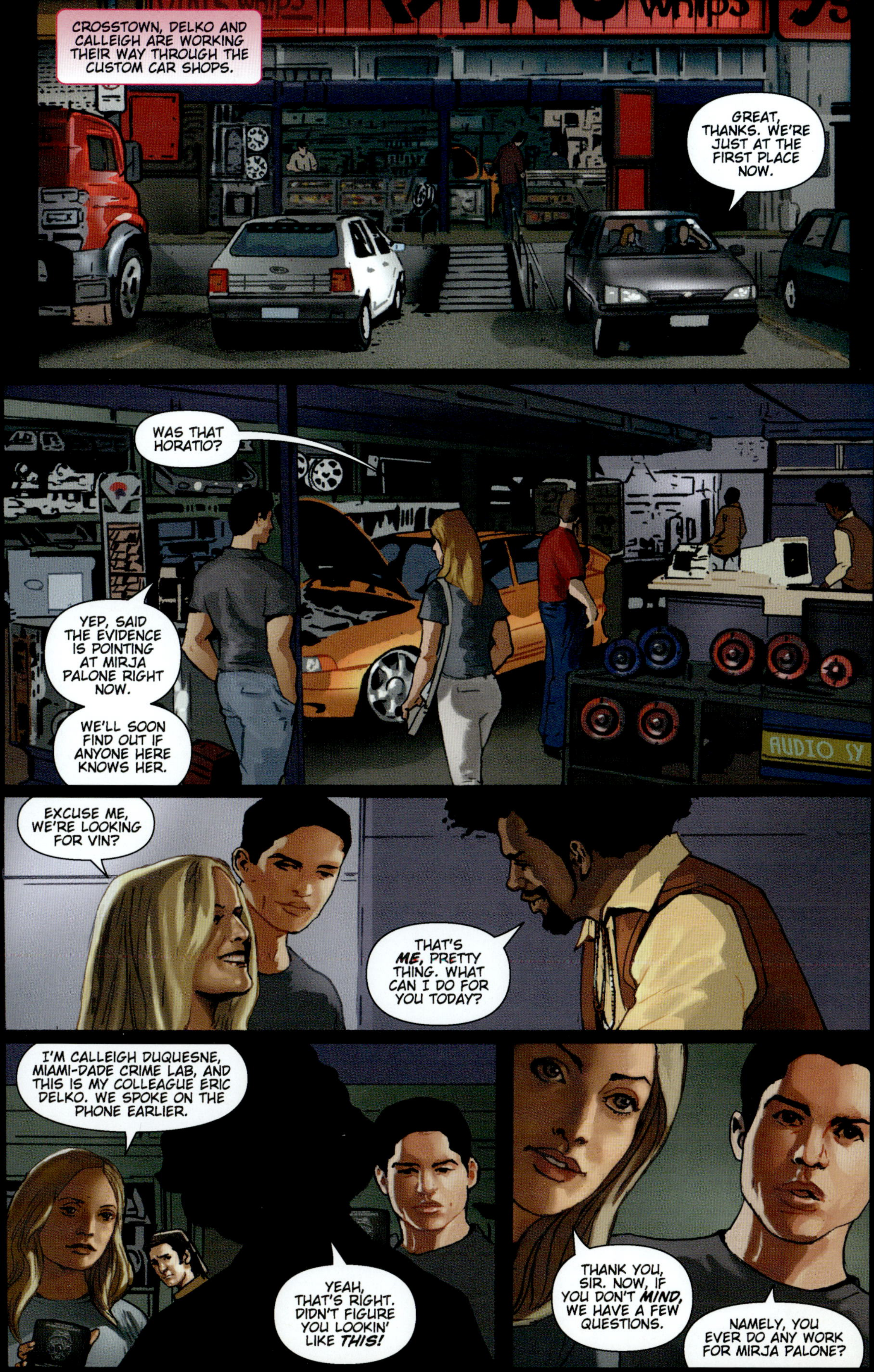
CROSSTOWN, DELKO AND CALLEIGH ARE WORKING THEIR WAY THROUGH THE CUSTOM CAR SHOPS.
GREAT, THANKS. WE'RE JUST AT THE FIRST PLACE NOW.
WAS THAT HORATIO?
YEP, SAID THE EVIDENCE IS POINTING AT MIRJA PALONE RIGHT NOW.
WE'LL SOON FIND OUT IF ANYONE HERE KNOWS HER.
AUDIO SY
EXCUSE ME, WE'RE LOOKING FOR VIN?
THAT'S *ME*, PRETTY THING. WHAT CAN I DO FOR YOU TODAY?
I'M CALLEIGH DUQUESNE, MIAMI-DADE CRIME LAB, AND THIS IS MY COLLEAGUE ERIC DELKO. WE SPOKE ON THE PHONE EARLIER.
YEAH, THAT'S RIGHT. DIDN'T FIGURE YOU LOOKIN' LIKE *THIS!*
THANK YOU, SIR. NOW, IF YOU DON'T *MIND*, WE HAVE A FEW QUESTIONS.
NAMELY, YOU EVER DO ANY WORK FOR MIRJA PALONE?

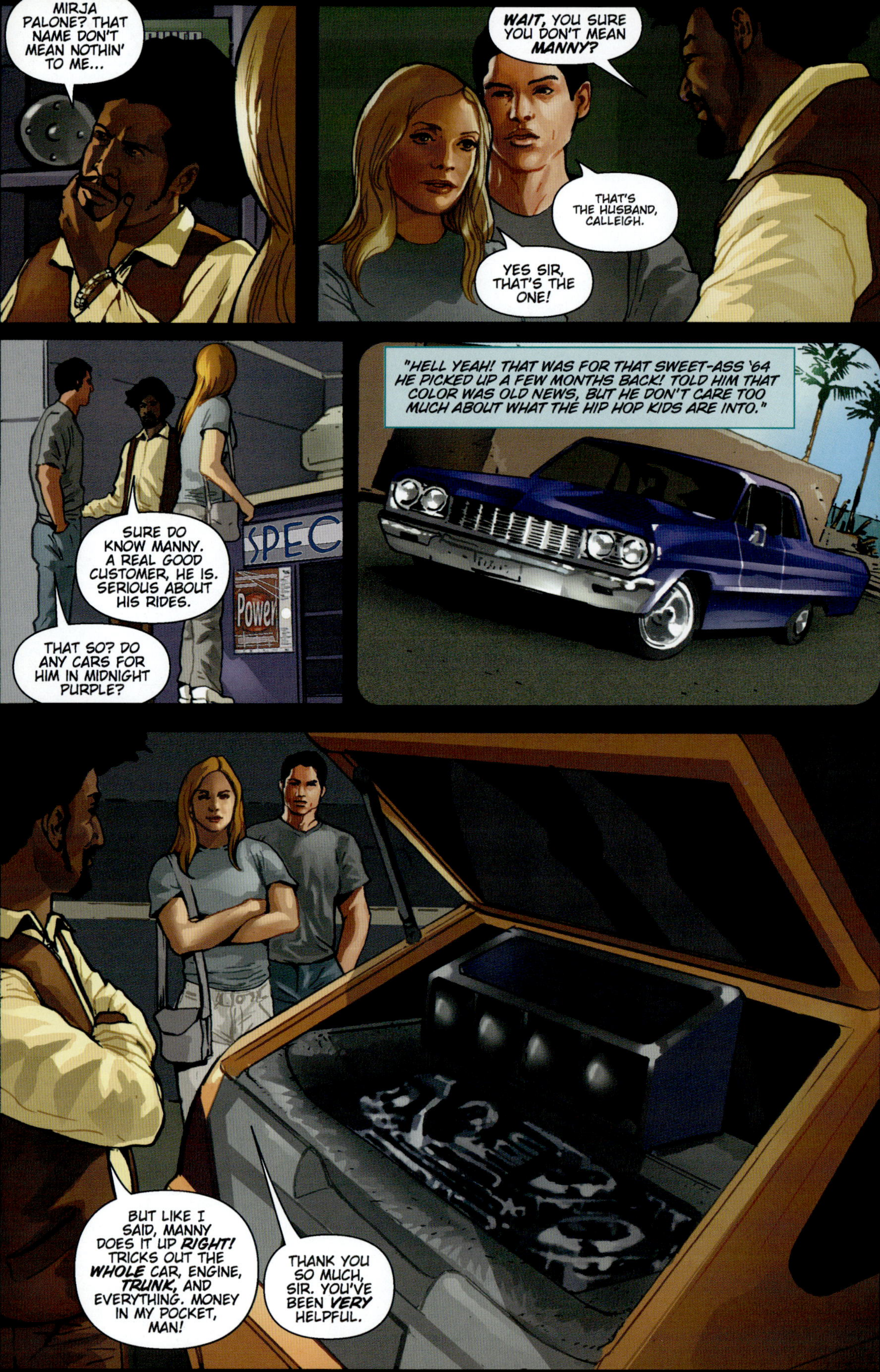
MIRJA PALONE? THAT NAME DON'T MEAN NOTHIN' TO ME...
WAIT, YOU SURE YOU DON'T MEAN MANNY?
THAT'S THE HUSBAND, CALLEIGH.
YES SIR, THAT'S THE ONE!
SPEC
Power
SURE DO KNOW MANNY. A REAL GOOD CUSTOMER, HE IS. SERIOUS ABOUT HIS RIDES.
THAT SO? DO ANY CARS FOR HIM IN MIDNIGHT PURPLE?
"HELL YEAH! THAT WAS FOR THAT SWEET-ASS '64 HE PICKED UP A FEW MONTHS BACK! TOLD HIM THAT COLOR WAS OLD NEWS, BUT HE DON'T CARE TOO MUCH ABOUT WHAT THE HIP HOP KIDS ARE INTO."
BUT LIKE I SAID, MANNY DOES IT UP RIGHT! TRICKS OUT THE WHOLE CAR, ENGINE, TRUNK, AND EVERYTHING. MONEY IN MY POCKET, MAN!
THANK YOU SO MUCH, SIR. YOU'VE BEEN VERY HELPFUL.

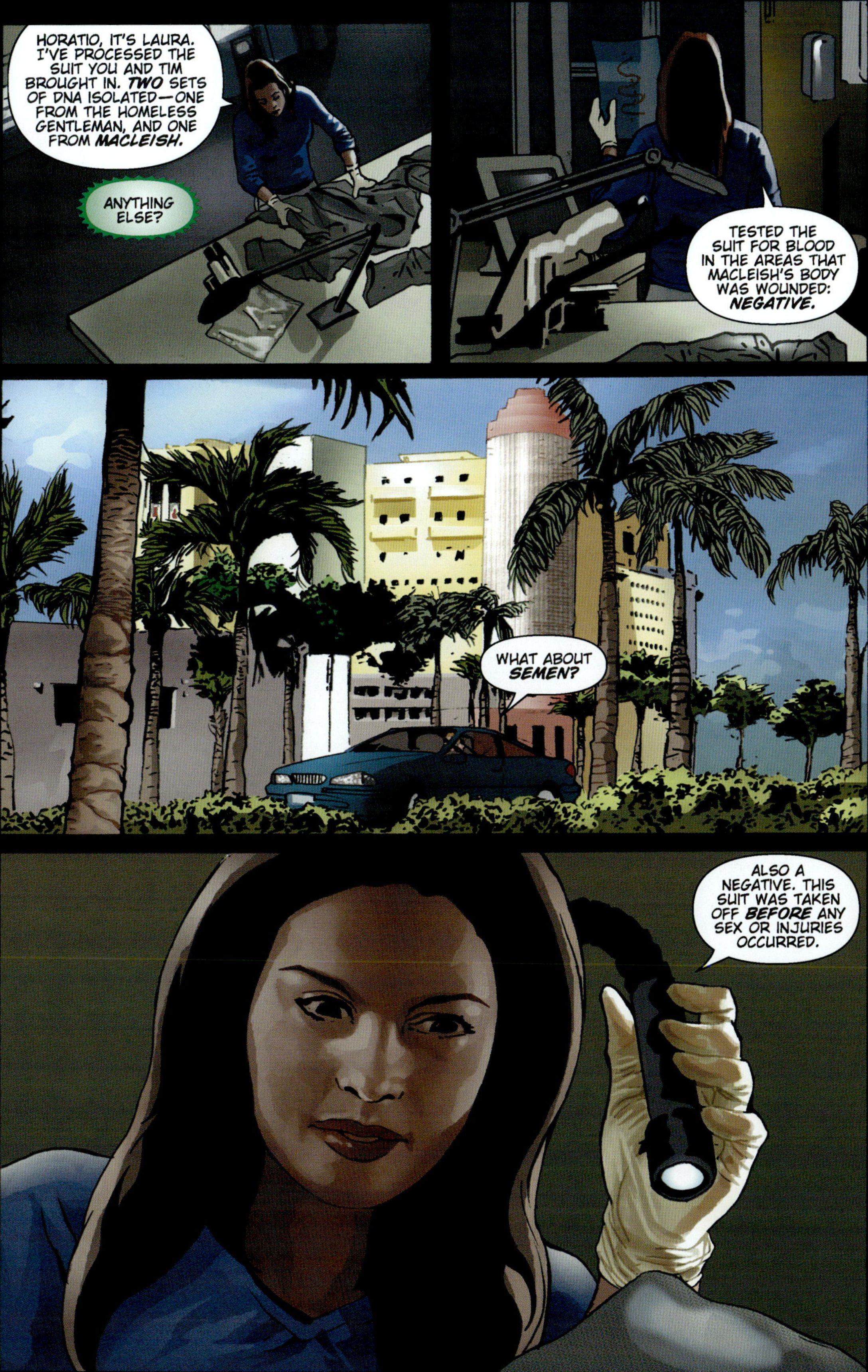
HORATIO, IT'S LAURA. I'VE PROCESSED THE SUIT YOU AND TIM BROUGHT IN. **TWO** SETS OF DNA ISOLATED—ONE FROM THE HOMELESS GENTLEMAN, AND ONE FROM **MACLEISH.**
ANYTHING ELSE?
TESTED THE SUIT FOR BLOOD IN THE AREAS THAT MACLEISH'S BODY WAS WOUNDED: **NEGATIVE.**
WHAT ABOUT **SEMEN?**
ALSO A NEGATIVE. THIS SUIT WAS TAKEN OFF **BEFORE** ANY SEX OR INJURIES OCCURRED.

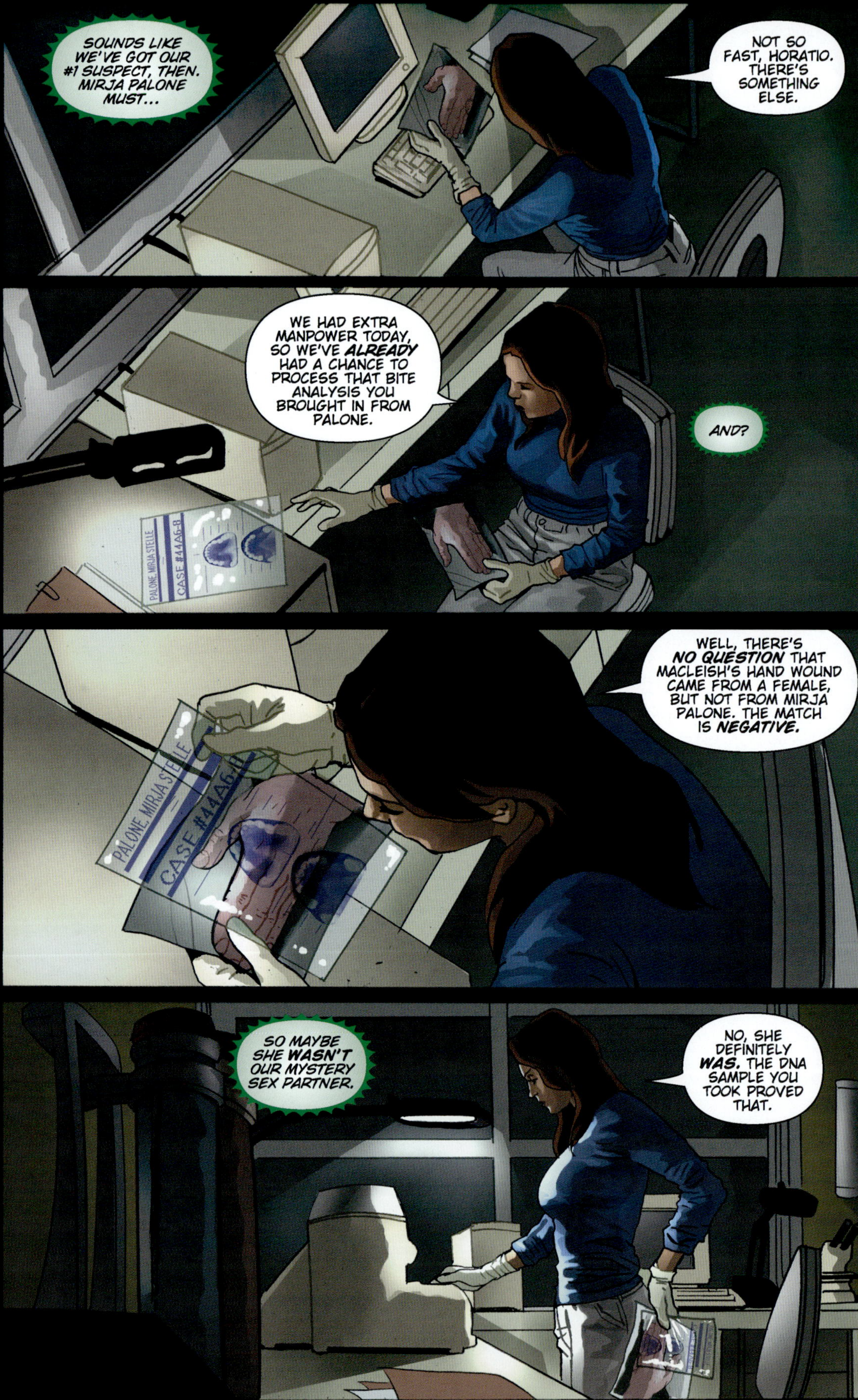
SOUNDS LIKE WE'VE GOT OUR #1 SUSPECT, THEN. MIRJA PALONE MUST...
NOT SO FAST, HORATIO. THERE'S SOMETHING ELSE.
WE HAD EXTRA MANPOWER TODAY, SO WE'VE **ALREADY** HAD A CHANCE TO PROCESS THAT BITE ANALYSIS YOU BROUGHT IN FROM PALONE.
AND?
PALONE, MIRJA STELLE
CASE #44A6-8
WELL, THERE'S **NO QUESTION** THAT MACLEISH'S HAND WOUND CAME FROM A FEMALE, BUT NOT FROM MIRJA PALONE. THE MATCH IS **NEGATIVE.**
SO MAYBE SHE **WASN'T** OUR MYSTERY SEX PARTNER.
NO, SHE DEFINITELY **WAS.** THE DNA SAMPLE YOU TOOK PROVED THAT.

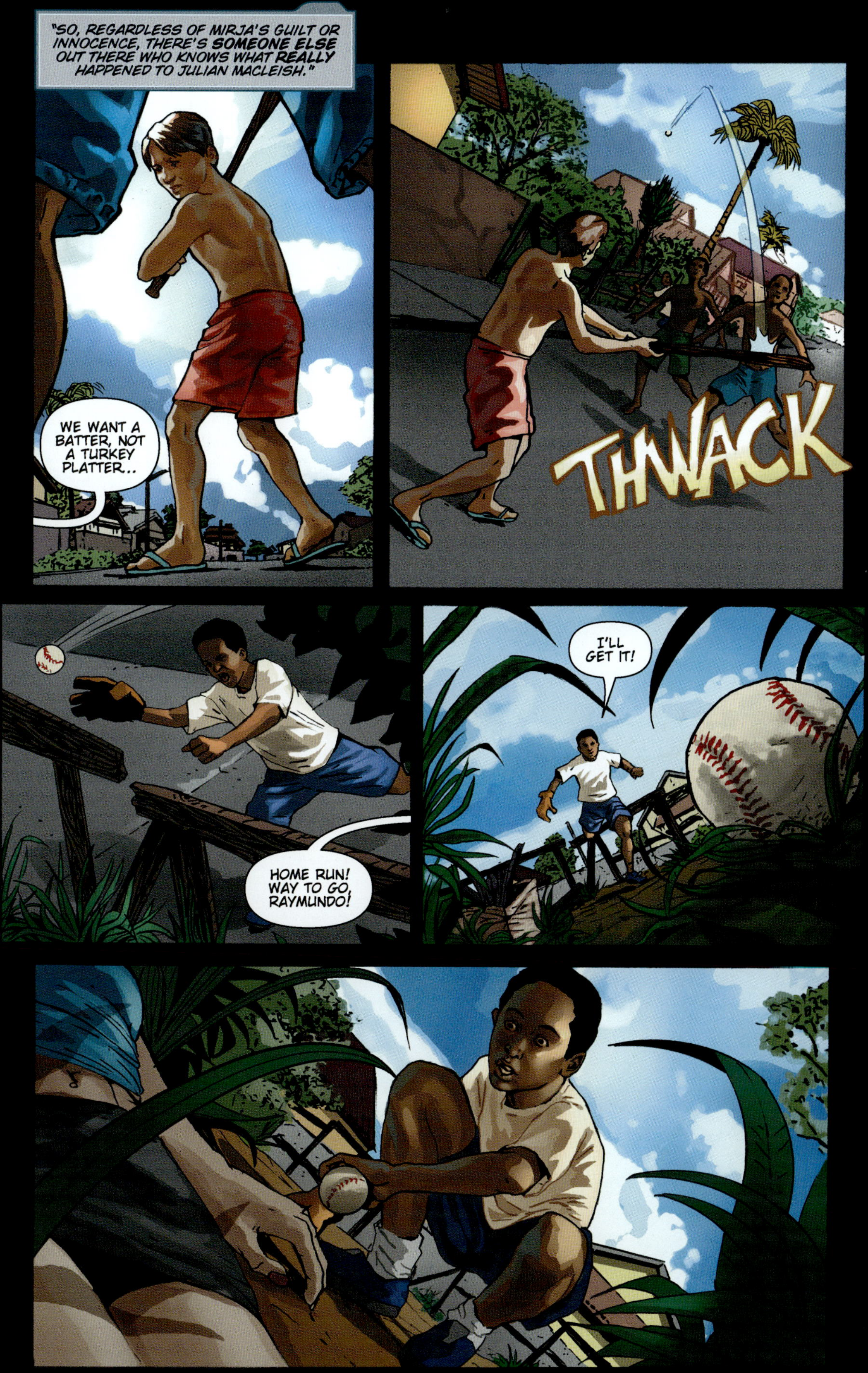

"SO, REGARDLESS OF MIRJA'S GUILT OR INNOCENCE, THERE'S SOMEONE ELSE OUT THERE WHO KNOWS WHAT REALLY HAPPENED TO JULIAN MACLEISH."
WE WANT A BATTER, NOT A TURKEY PLATTER..
THWACK
HOME RUN! WAY TO GO, RAYMUNDO!
I'LL GET IT!

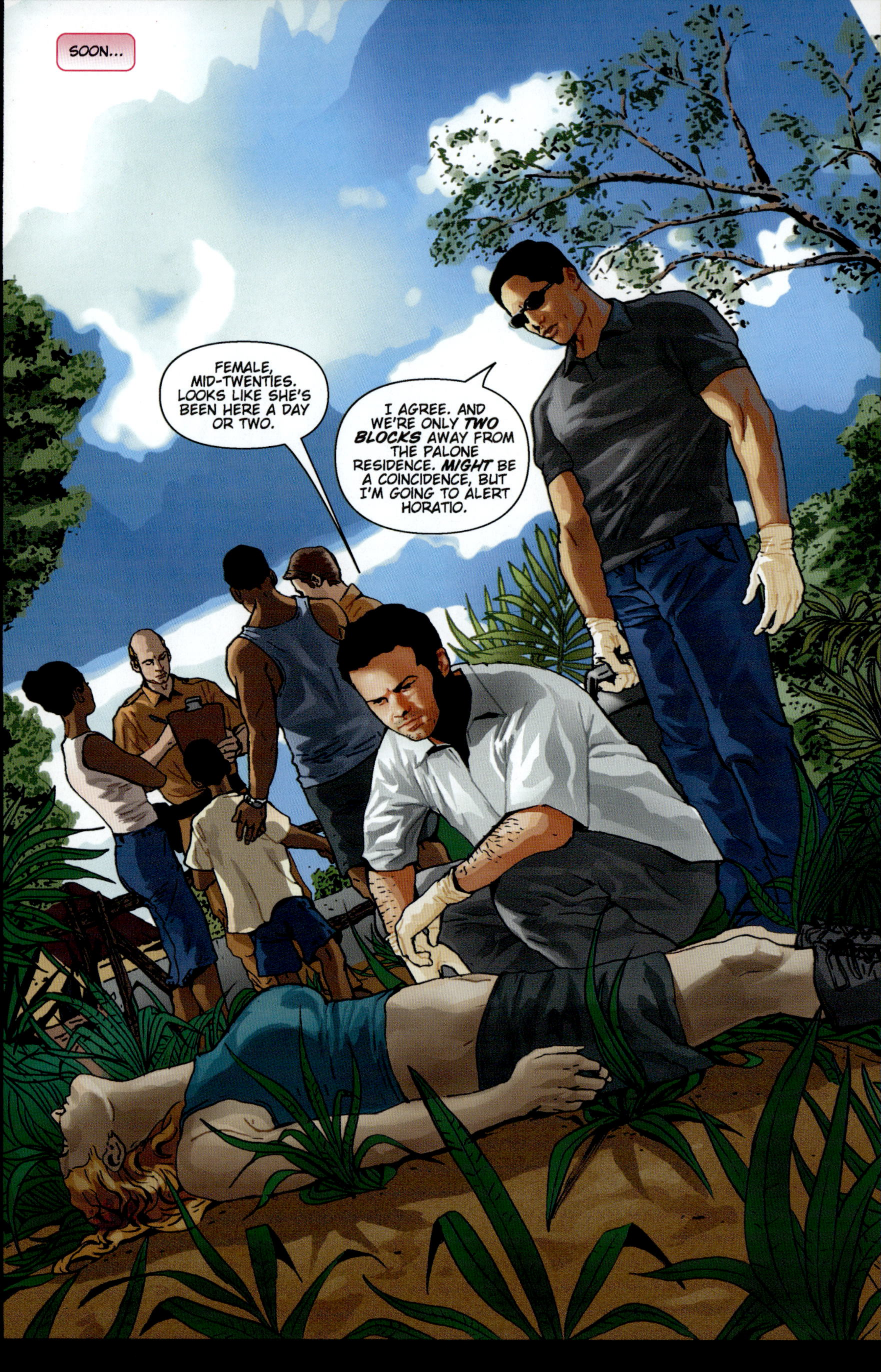
SOON...
FEMALE, MID-TWENTIES. LOOKS LIKE SHE'S BEEN HERE A DAY OR TWO.
I AGREE. AND WE'RE ONLY **TWO BLOCKS** AWAY FROM THE PALONE RESIDENCE. ***MIGHT*** BE A COINCIDENCE, BUT I'M GOING TO ALERT HORATIO.

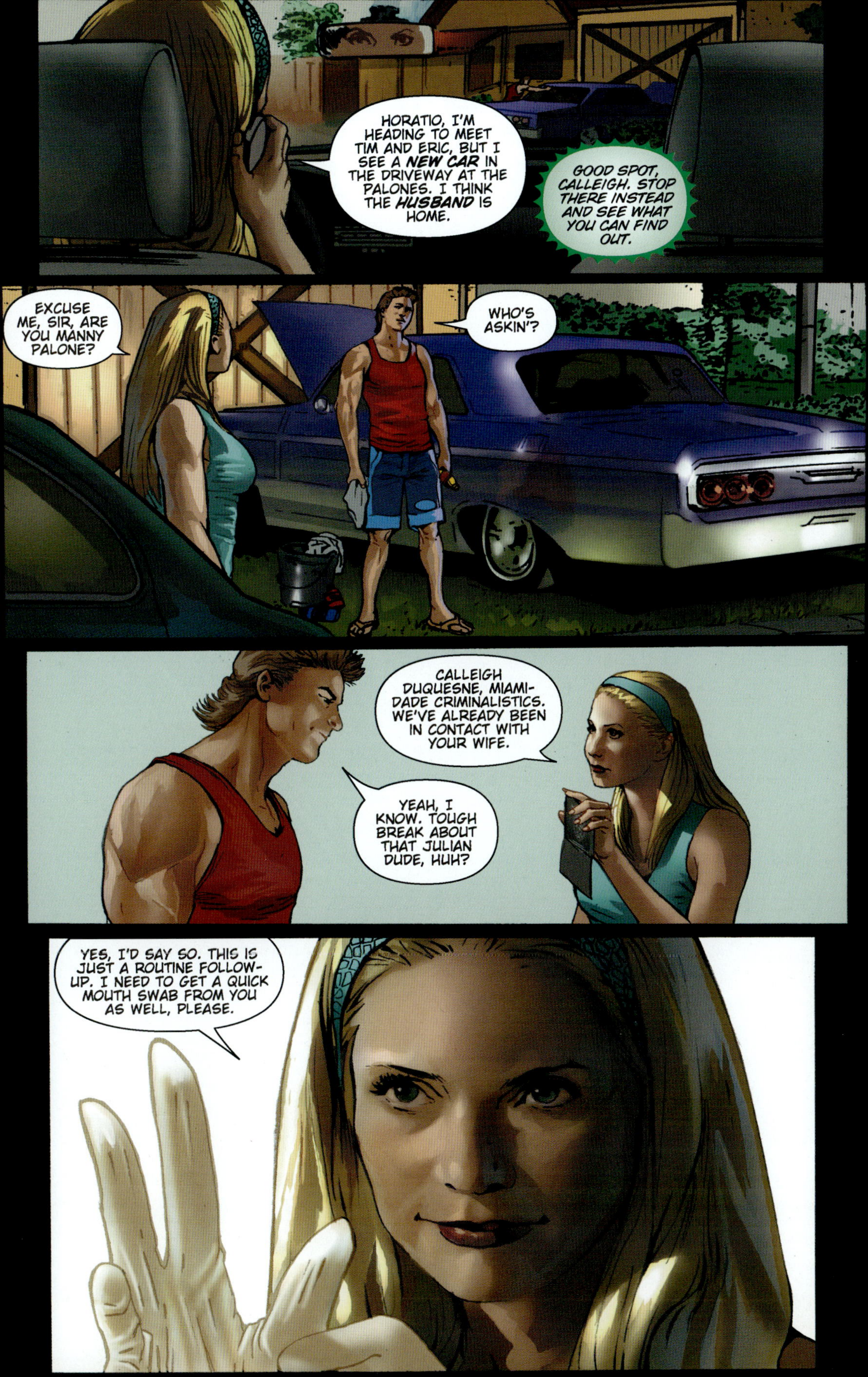

HORATIO, I'M HEADING TO MEET TIM AND ERIC, BUT I SEE A **NEW CAR** IN THE DRIVEWAY AT THE PALONES. I THINK THE **HUSBAND** IS HOME.
GOOD SPOT, CALLEIGH. STOP THERE INSTEAD AND SEE WHAT YOU CAN FIND OUT.
EXCUSE ME, SIR, ARE YOU MANNY PALONE?
WHO'S ASKIN'?
CALLEIGH DUQUESNE, MIAMI-DADE CRIMINALISTICS. WE'VE ALREADY BEEN IN CONTACT WITH YOUR WIFE.
YEAH, I KNOW. TOUGH BREAK ABOUT THAT JULIAN DUDE, HUH?
YES, I'D SAY SO. THIS IS JUST A ROUTINE FOLLOW-UP. I NEED TO GET A QUICK MOUTH SWAB FROM YOU AS WELL, PLEASE.

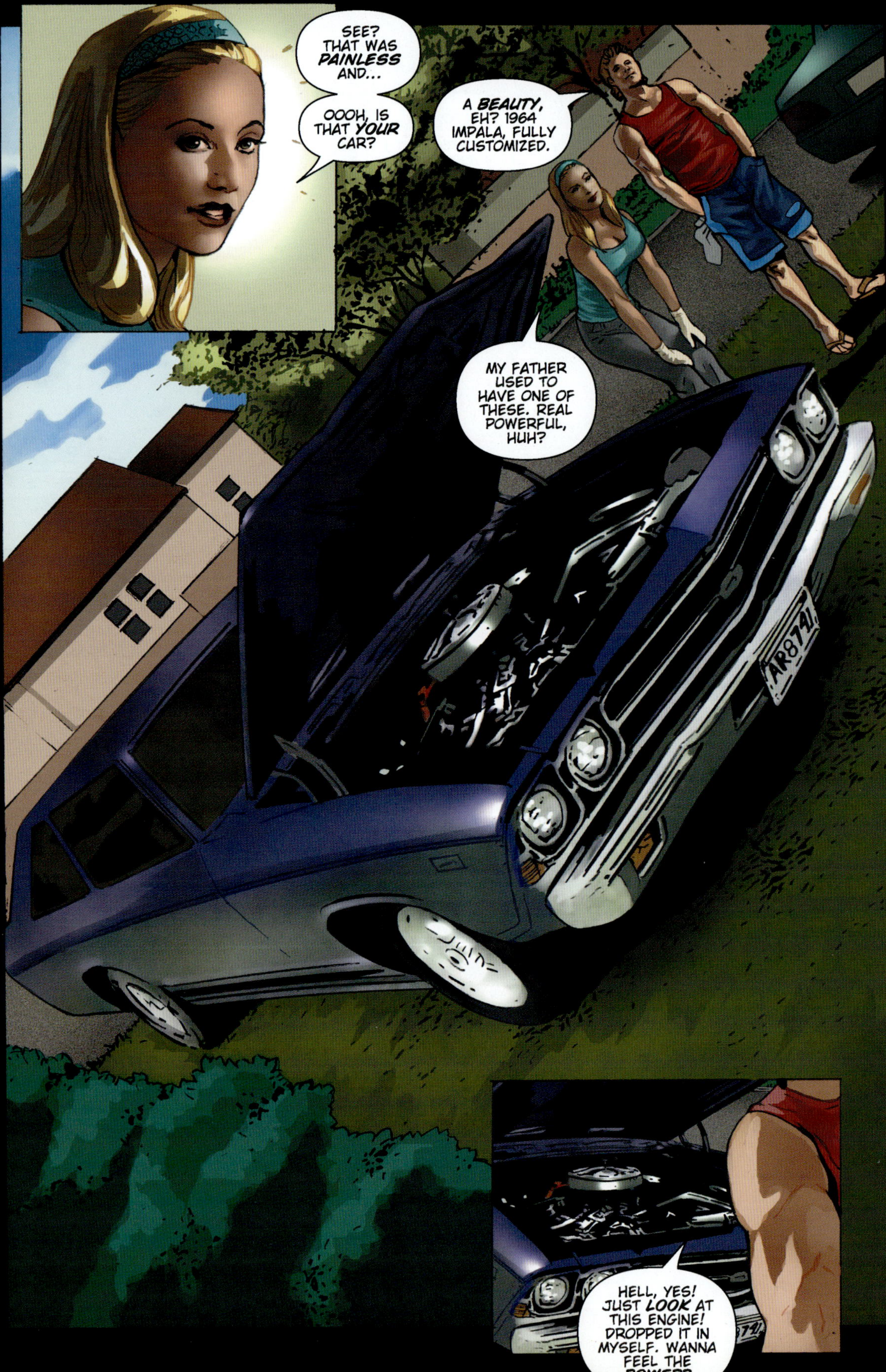
SEE? THAT WAS PAINLESS AND...
OOOH, IS THAT YOUR CAR?
A BEAUTY, EH? 1964 IMPALA, FULLY CUSTOMIZED.
MY FATHER USED TO HAVE ONE OF THESE. REAL POWERFUL, HUH?
AR8741
HELL, YES! JUST LOOK AT THIS ENGINE! DROPPED IT IN MYSELF. WANNA FEEL THE POWER?

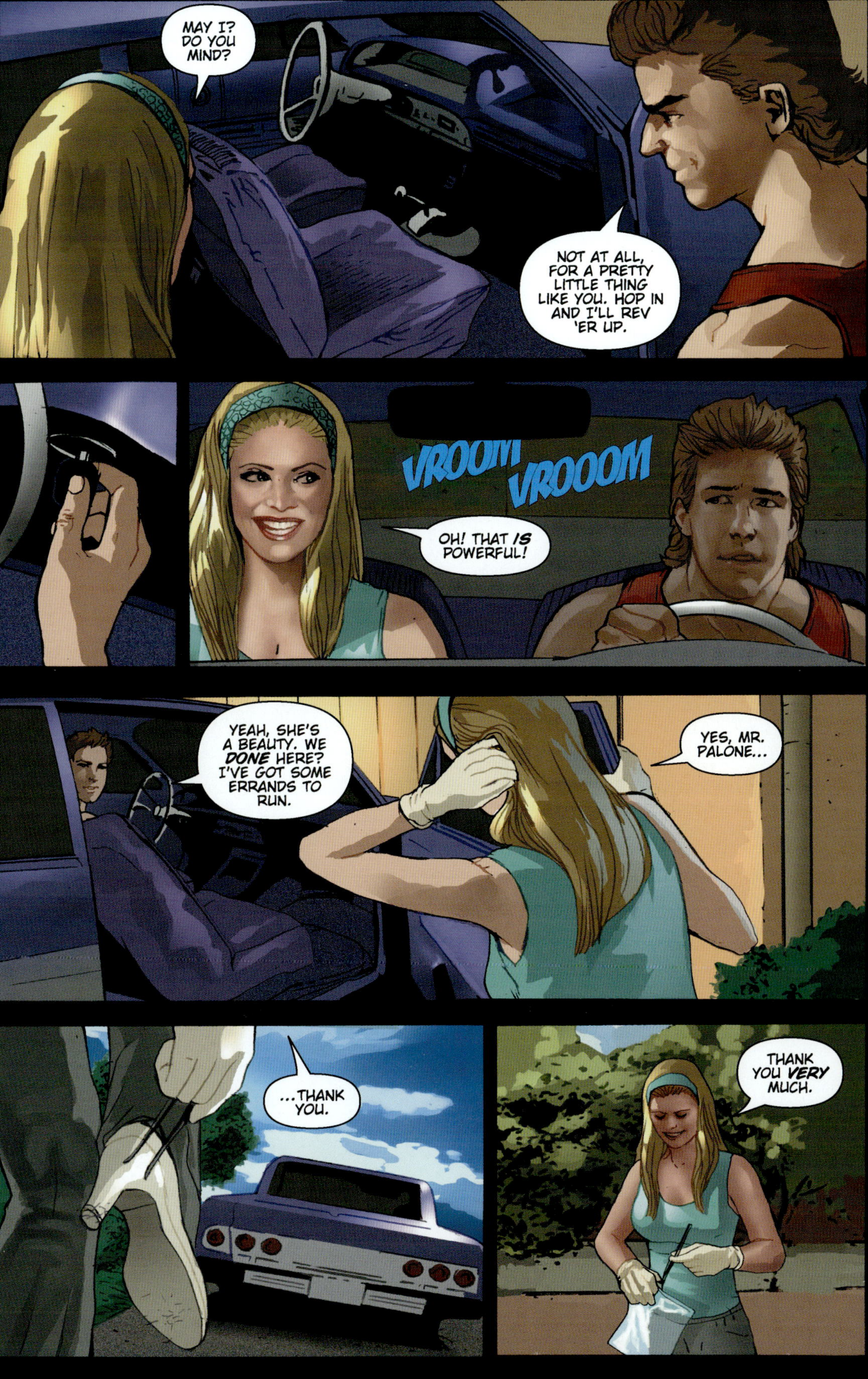
MAY I? DO YOU MIND?
NOT AT ALL, FOR A PRETTY LITTLE THING LIKE YOU. HOP IN AND I'LL REV 'ER UP.
VROOM VROOOM
OH! THAT *IS* POWERFUL!
YEAH, SHE'S A BEAUTY. WE *DONE* HERE? I'VE GOT SOME ERRANDS TO RUN.
YES, MR. PALONE...
...THANK YOU.
THANK YOU *VERY* MUCH.

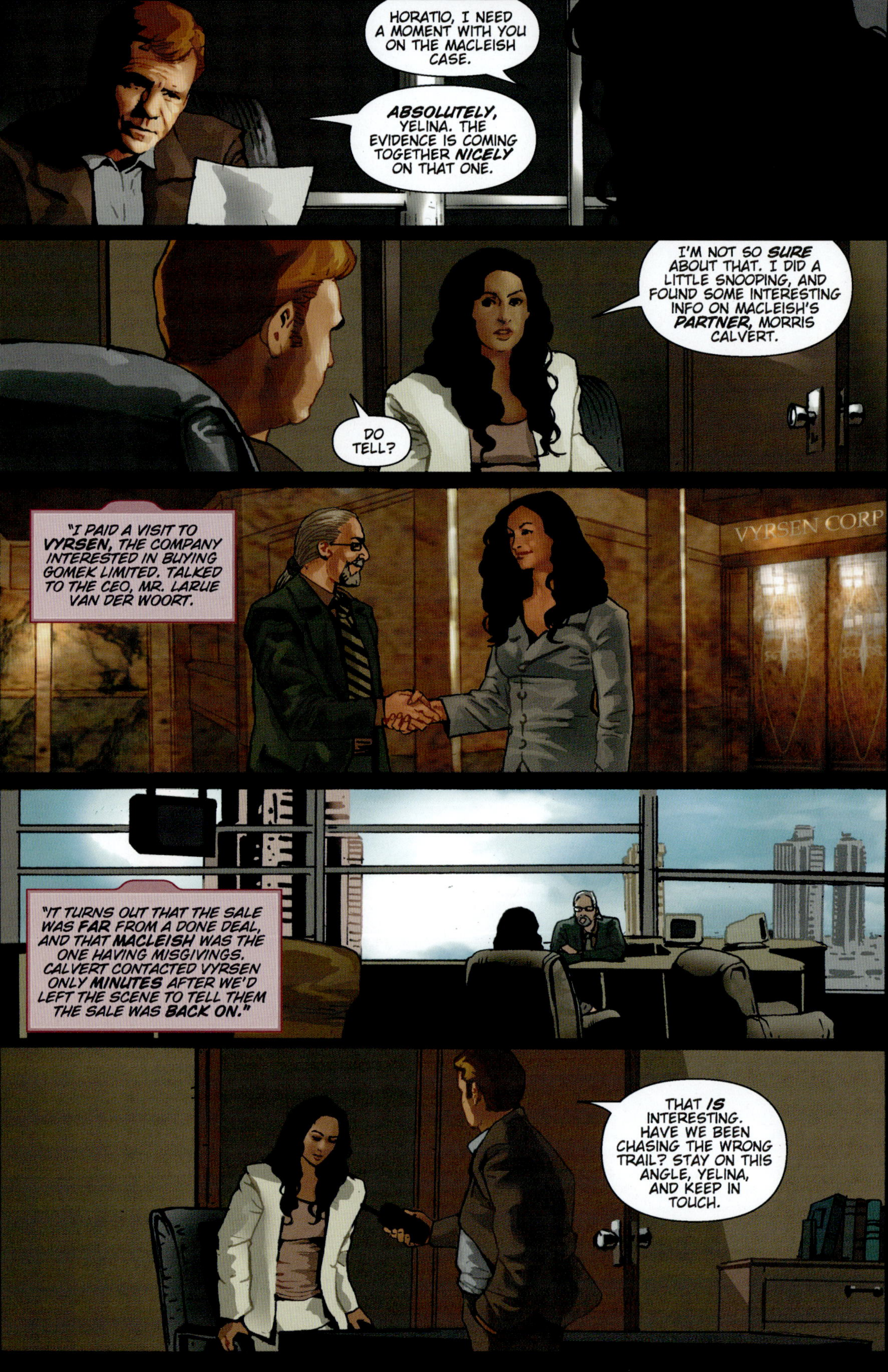
HORATIO, I NEED A MOMENT WITH YOU ON THE MACLEISH CASE.
ABSOLUTELY, YELINA. THE EVIDENCE IS COMING TOGETHER NICELY ON THAT ONE.
I'M NOT SO SURE ABOUT THAT. I DID A LITTLE SNOOPING, AND FOUND SOME INTERESTING INFO ON MACLEISH'S PARTNER, MORRIS CALVERT.
DO TELL?
"I PAID A VISIT TO VYRSEN, THE COMPANY INTERESTED IN BUYING GOMEK LIMITED. TALKED TO THE CEO, MR. LARUE VAN DER WOORT.
VYRSEN CORP
"IT TURNS OUT THAT THE SALE WAS FAR FROM A DONE DEAL, AND THAT MACLEISH WAS THE ONE HAVING MISGIVINGS. CALVERT CONTACTED VYRSEN ONLY MINUTES AFTER WE'D LEFT THE SCENE TO TELL THEM THE SALE WAS BACK ON."
THAT IS INTERESTING. HAVE WE BEEN CHASING THE WRONG TRAIL? STAY ON THIS ANGLE, YELINA, AND KEEP IN TOUCH.

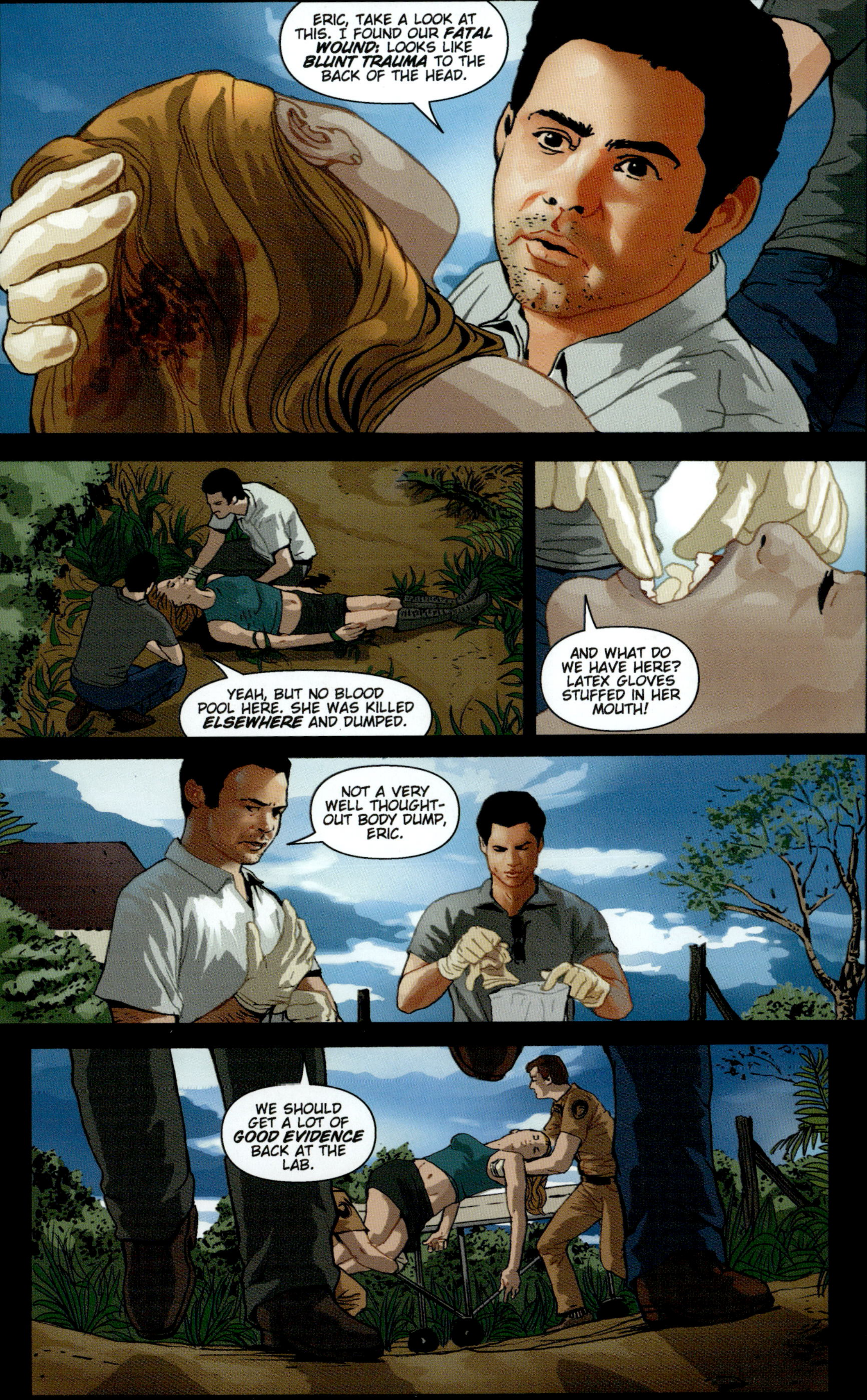
ERIC, TAKE A LOOK AT THIS. I FOUND OUR *FATAL WOUND*: LOOKS LIKE *BLUNT TRAUMA* TO THE BACK OF THE HEAD.
YEAH, BUT NO BLOOD POOL HERE. SHE WAS KILLED *ELSEWHERE* AND DUMPED.
AND WHAT DO WE HAVE HERE? LATEX GLOVES STUFFED IN HER MOUTH!
NOT A VERY WELL THOUGHT-OUT BODY DUMP, ERIC.
WE SHOULD GET A LOT OF *GOOD EVIDENCE* BACK AT THE LAB.

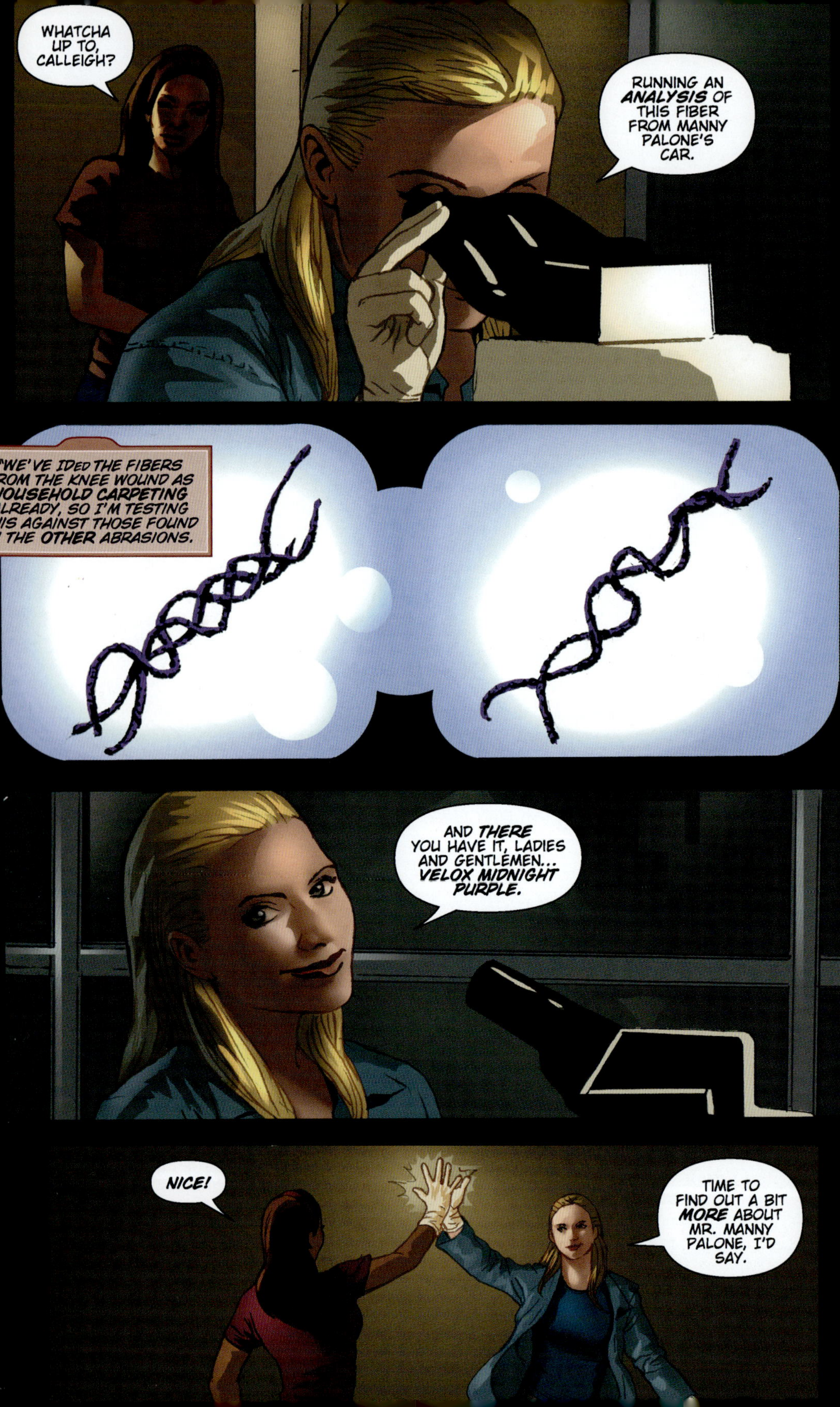
WHATCHA UP TO, CALLEIGH?
RUNNING AN ANALYSIS OF THIS FIBER FROM MANNY PALONE'S CAR.
"WE'VE IDED THE FIBERS FROM THE KNEE WOUND AS HOUSEHOLD CARPETING ALREADY, SO I'M TESTING THIS AGAINST THOSE FOUND IN THE OTHER ABRASIONS.
AND THERE YOU HAVE IT, LADIES AND GENTLEMEN... VELOX MIDNIGHT PURPLE.
NICE!
TIME TO FIND OUT A BIT MORE ABOUT MR. MANNY PALONE, I'D SAY.

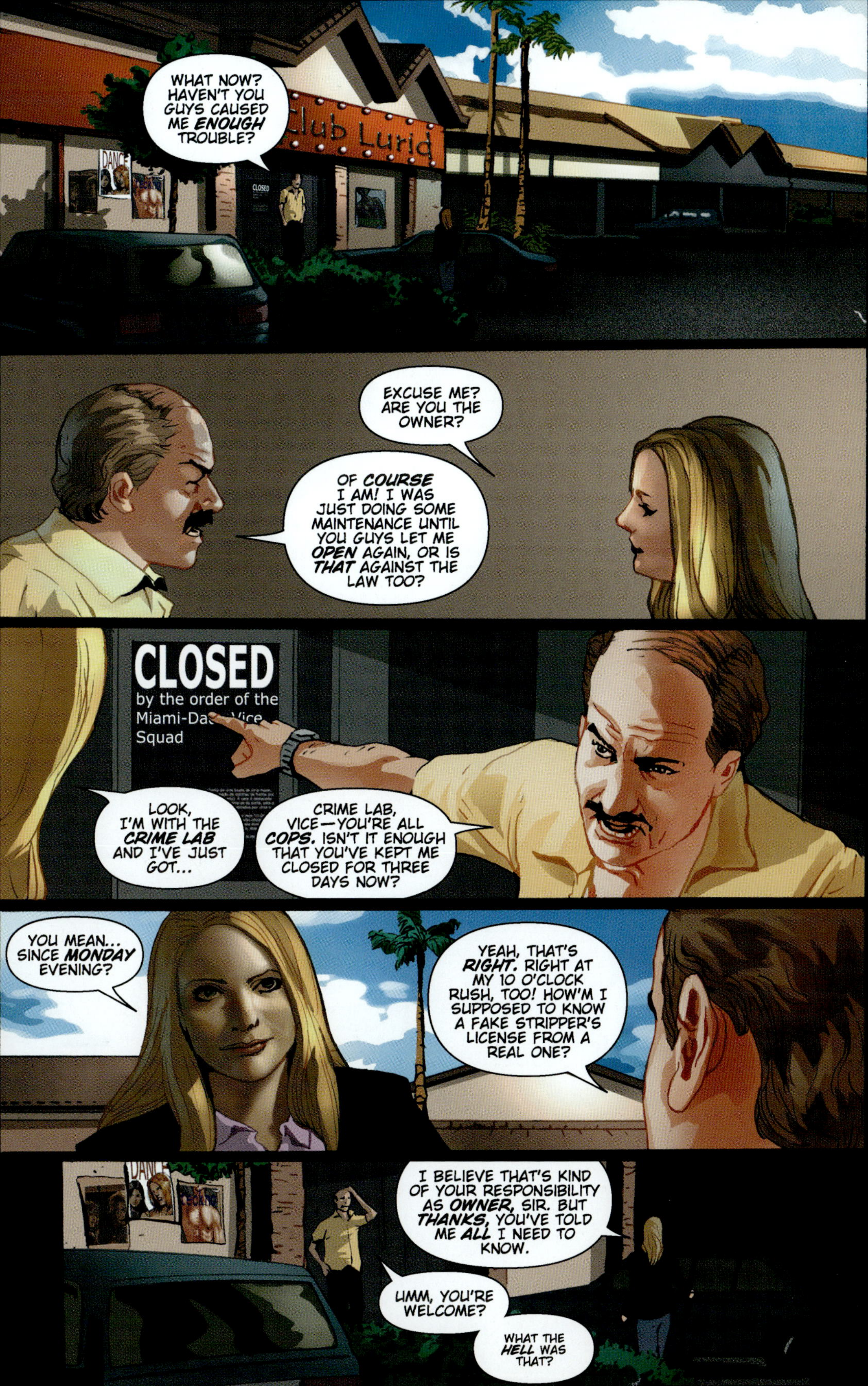
Club Lurid
WHAT NOW? HAVEN'T YOU GUYS CAUSED ME ENOUGH TROUBLE?
EXCUSE ME? ARE YOU THE OWNER?
OF COURSE I AM! I WAS JUST DOING SOME MAINTENANCE UNTIL YOU GUYS LET ME OPEN AGAIN, OR IS THAT AGAINST THE LAW TOO?
CLOSED
by the order of the Miami-Dade Vice Squad
LOOK, I'M WITH THE CRIME LAB AND I'VE JUST GOT...
CRIME LAB, VICE—YOU'RE ALL COPS. ISN'T IT ENOUGH THAT YOU'VE KEPT ME CLOSED FOR THREE DAYS NOW?
YOU MEAN... SINCE MONDAY EVENING?
YEAH, THAT'S RIGHT. RIGHT AT MY 10 O'CLOCK RUSH, TOO! HOW'M I SUPPOSED TO KNOW A FAKE STRIPPER'S LICENSE FROM A REAL ONE?
I BELIEVE THAT'S KIND OF YOUR RESPONSIBILITY AS OWNER, SIR. BUT THANKS, YOU'VE TOLD ME ALL I NEED TO KNOW.
UMM, YOU'RE WELCOME?
WHAT THE HELL WAS THAT?

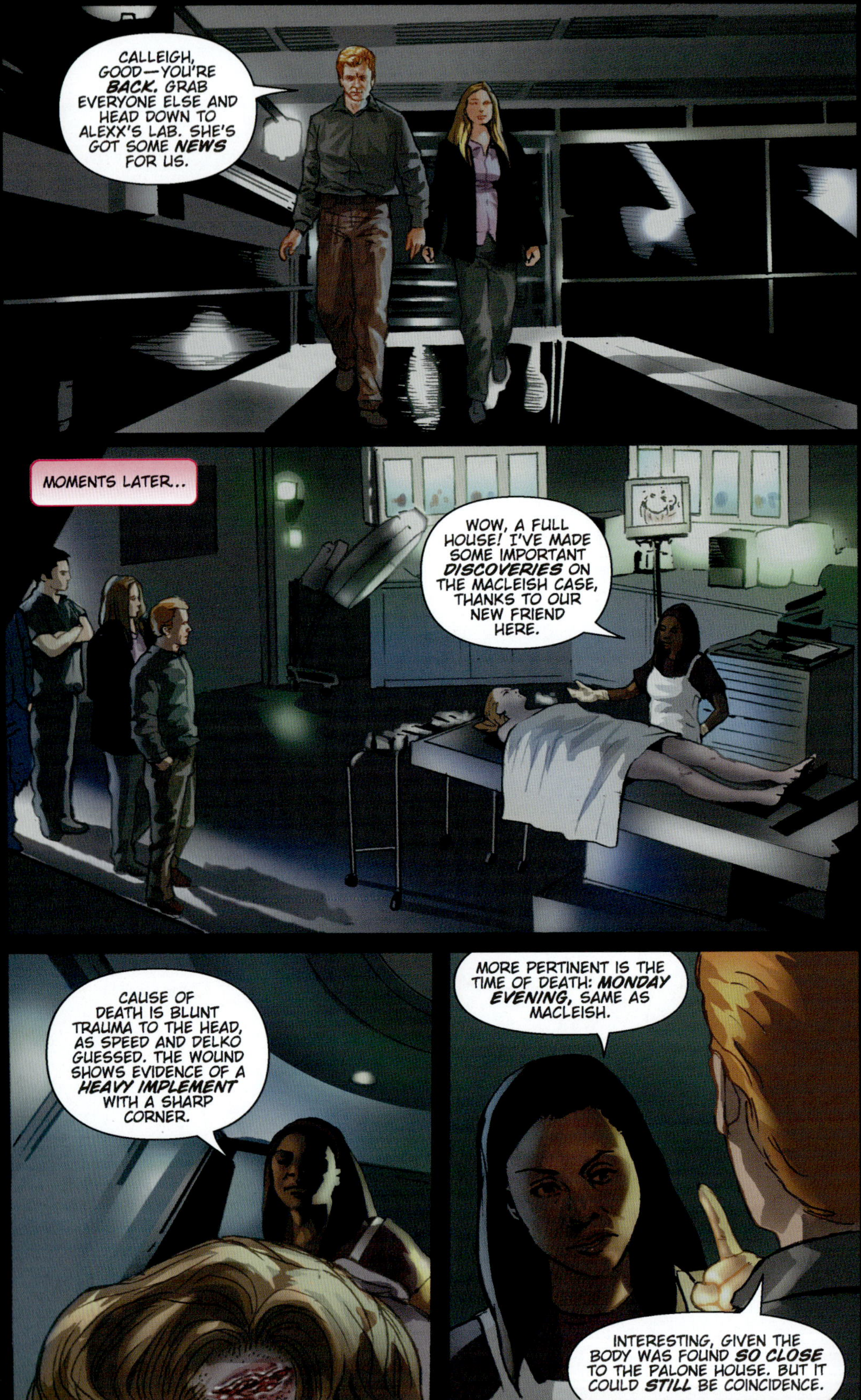
CALLEIGH, GOOD—YOU'RE BACK. GRAB EVERYONE ELSE AND HEAD DOWN TO ALEXX'S LAB. SHE'S GOT SOME NEWS FOR US.
MOMENTS LATER...
WOW, A FULL HOUSE! I'VE MADE SOME IMPORTANT DISCOVERIES ON THE MACLEISH CASE, THANKS TO OUR NEW FRIEND HERE.
CAUSE OF DEATH IS BLUNT TRAUMA TO THE HEAD, AS SPEED AND DELKO GUESSED. THE WOUND SHOWS EVIDENCE OF A HEAVY IMPLEMENT WITH A SHARP CORNER.
MORE PERTINENT IS THE TIME OF DEATH: MONDAY EVENING, SAME AS MACLEISH.
INTERESTING, GIVEN THE BODY WAS FOUND SO CLOSE TO THE PALONE HOUSE. BUT IT COULD STILL BE COINCIDENCE.

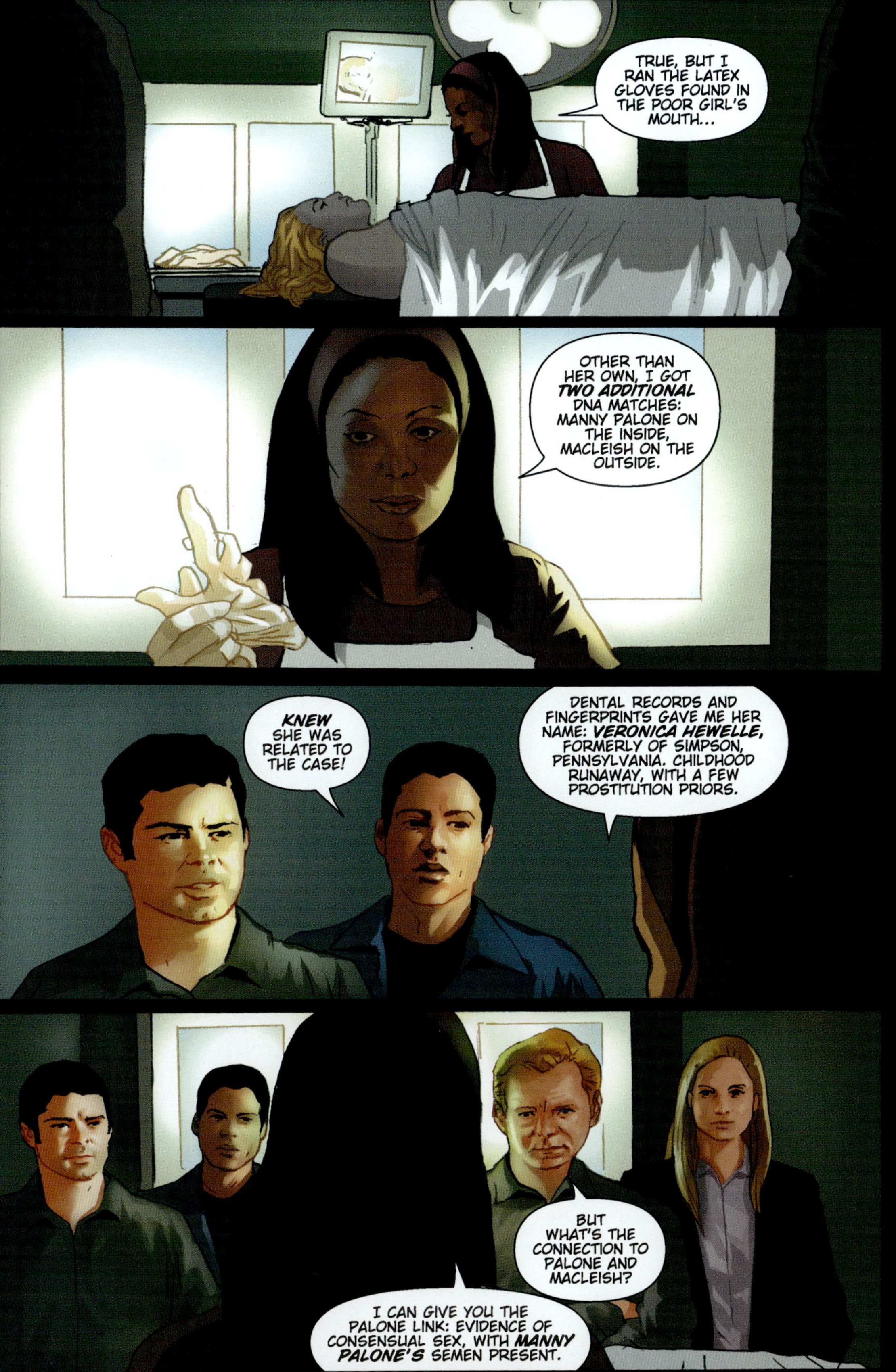
TRUE, BUT I RAN THE LATEX GLOVES FOUND IN THE POOR GIRL'S MOUTH...
OTHER THAN HER OWN, I GOT TWO ADDITIONAL DNA MATCHES: MANNY PALONE ON THE INSIDE, MACLEISH ON THE OUTSIDE.
KNEW SHE WAS RELATED TO THE CASE!
DENTAL RECORDS AND FINGERPRINTS GAVE ME HER NAME: VERONICA HEWELLE, FORMERLY OF SIMPSON, PENNSYLVANIA. CHILDHOOD RUNAWAY, WITH A FEW PROSTITUTION PRIORS.
BUT WHAT'S THE CONNECTION TO PALONE AND MACLEISH?
I CAN GIVE YOU THE PALONE LINK: EVIDENCE OF CONSENSUAL SEX, WITH MANNY PALONE'S SEMEN PRESENT.

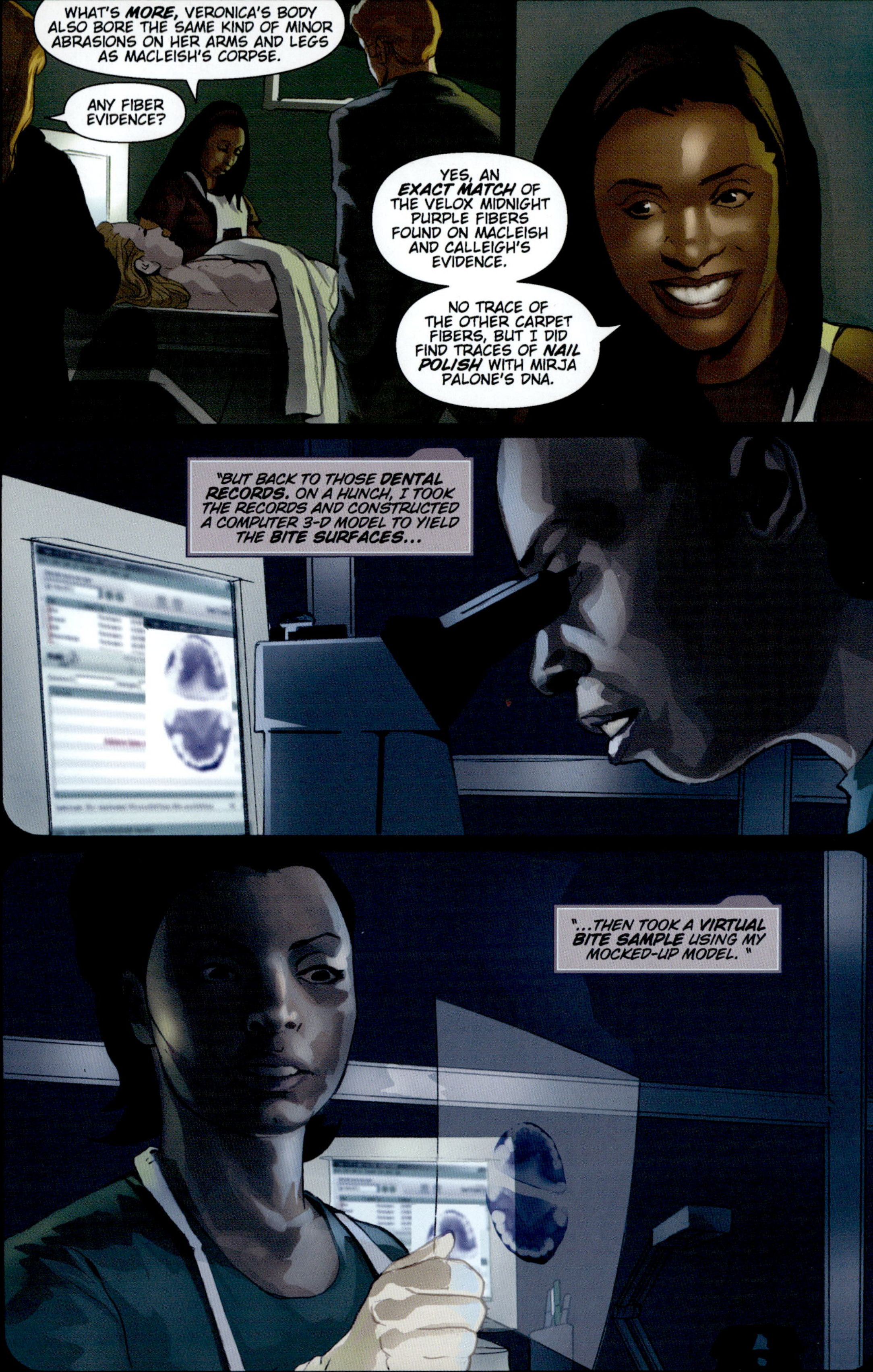
WHAT'S MORE, VERONICA'S BODY ALSO BORE THE SAME KIND OF MINOR ABRASIONS ON HER ARMS AND LEGS AS MACLEISH'S CORPSE.
ANY FIBER EVIDENCE?
YES, AN EXACT MATCH OF THE VELOX MIDNIGHT PURPLE FIBERS FOUND ON MACLEISH AND CALLEIGH'S EVIDENCE.
NO TRACE OF THE OTHER CARPET FIBERS, BUT I DID FIND TRACES OF NAIL POLISH WITH MIRJA PALONE'S DNA.
"BUT BACK TO THOSE DENTAL RECORDS. ON A HUNCH, I TOOK THE RECORDS AND CONSTRUCTED A COMPUTER 3-D MODEL TO YIELD THE BITE SURFACES...
"...THEN TOOK A VIRTUAL BITE SAMPLE USING MY MOCKED-UP MODEL."

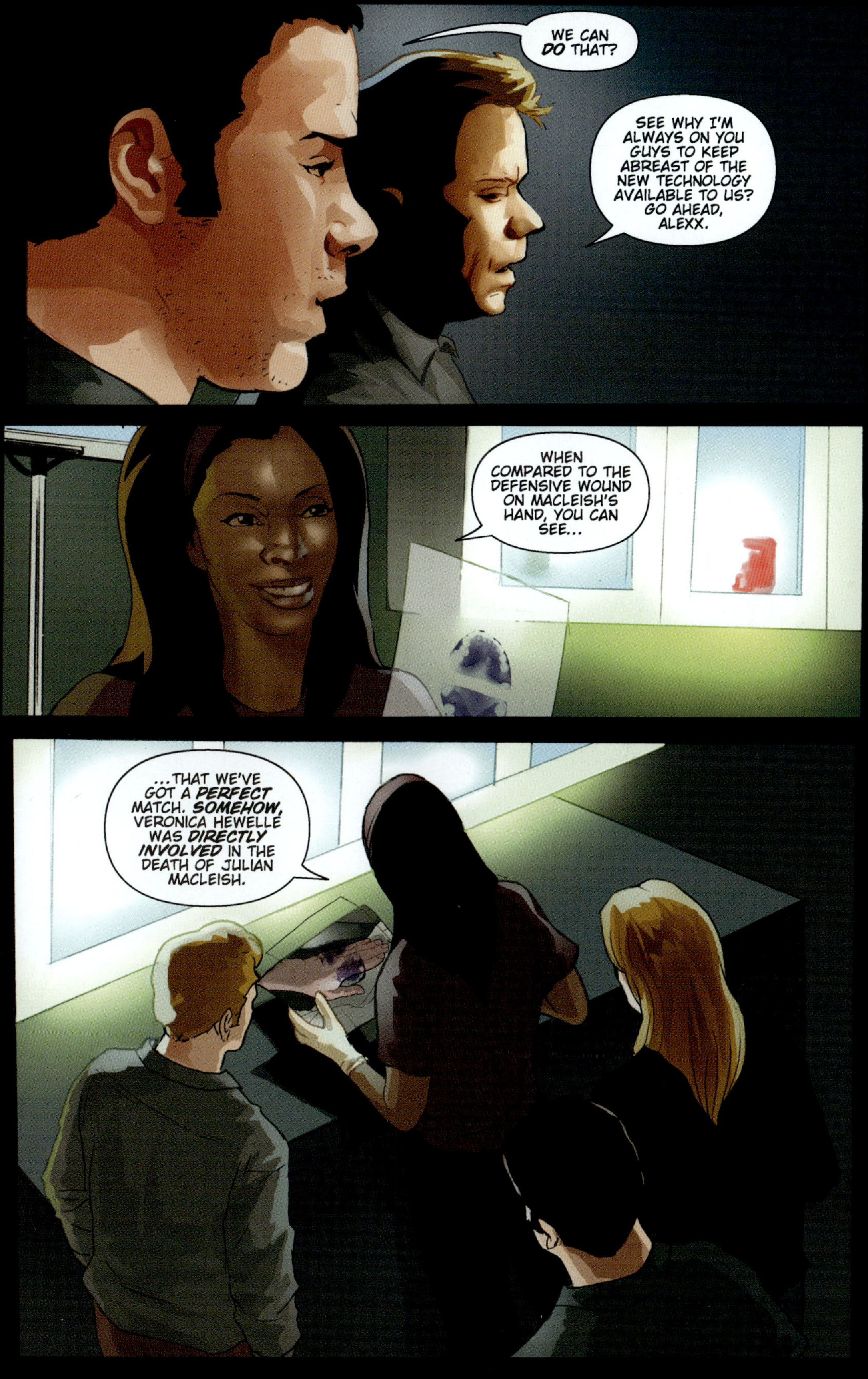
WE CAN DO THAT?
SEE WHY I'M ALWAYS ON YOU GUYS TO KEEP ABREAST OF THE NEW TECHNOLOGY AVAILABLE TO US? GO AHEAD, ALEXX.
WHEN COMPARED TO THE DEFENSIVE WOUND ON MACLEISH'S HAND, YOU CAN SEE...
...THAT WE'VE GOT A PERFECT MATCH. SOMEHOW, VERONICA HEWELLE WAS DIRECTLY INVOLVED IN THE DEATH OF JULIAN MACLEISH.

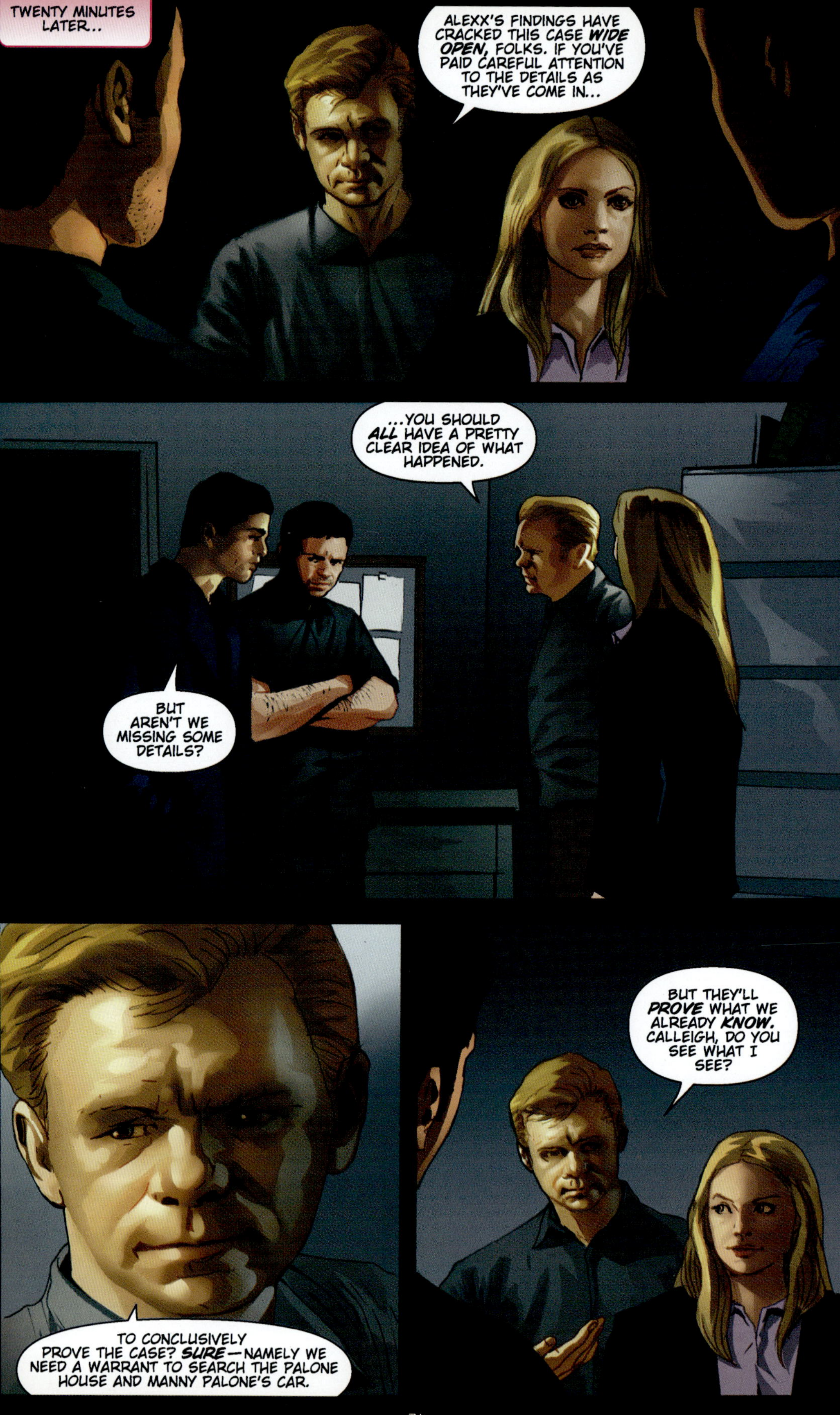

TWENTY MINUTES LATER...
ALEXX'S FINDINGS HAVE CRACKED THIS CASE WIDE OPEN, FOLKS. IF YOU'VE PAID CAREFUL ATTENTION TO THE DETAILS AS THEY'VE COME IN...
...YOU SHOULD ALL HAVE A PRETTY CLEAR IDEA OF WHAT HAPPENED.
BUT AREN'T WE MISSING SOME DETAILS?
TO CONCLUSIVELY PROVE THE CASE? SURE—NAMELY WE NEED A WARRANT TO SEARCH THE PALONE HOUSE AND MANNY PALONE'S CAR.
BUT THEY'LL PROVE WHAT WE ALREADY KNOW. CALLEIGH, DO YOU SEE WHAT I SEE?

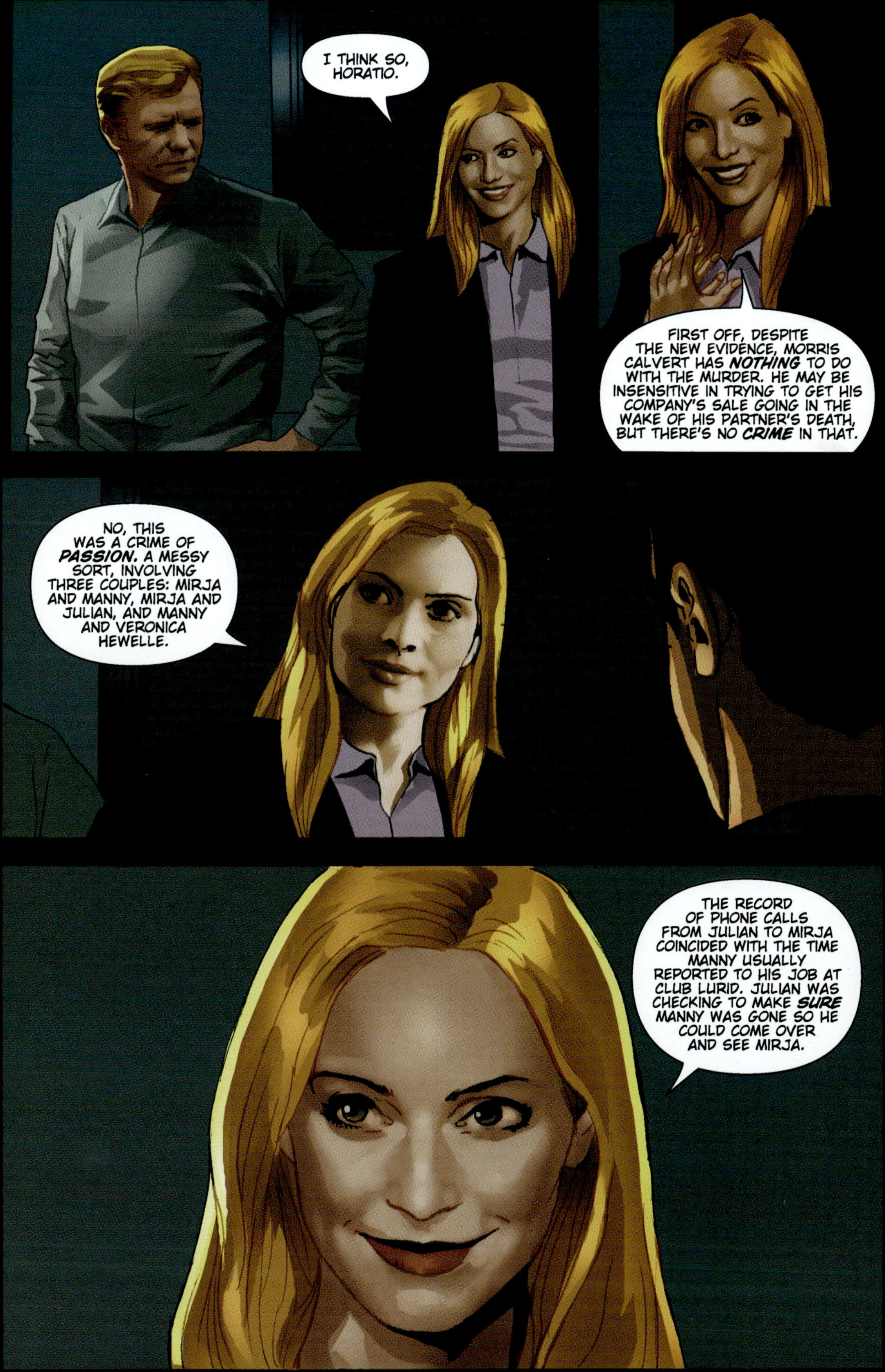
I THINK SO, HORATIO.
FIRST OFF, DESPITE THE NEW EVIDENCE, MORRIS CALVERT HAS *NOTHING* TO DO WITH THE MURDER. HE MAY BE INSENSITIVE IN TRYING TO GET HIS COMPANY'S SALE GOING IN THE WAKE OF HIS PARTNER'S DEATH, BUT THERE'S NO *CRIME* IN THAT.
NO, THIS WAS A CRIME OF *PASSION.* A MESSY SORT, INVOLVING THREE COUPLES: MIRJA AND MANNY, MIRJA AND JULIAN, AND MANNY AND VERONICA HEWELLE.
THE RECORD OF PHONE CALLS FROM JULIAN TO MIRJA COINCIDED WITH THE TIME MANNY USUALLY REPORTED TO HIS JOB AT CLUB LURID. JULIAN WAS CHECKING TO MAKE *SURE* MANNY WAS GONE SO HE COULD COME OVER AND SEE MIRJA.

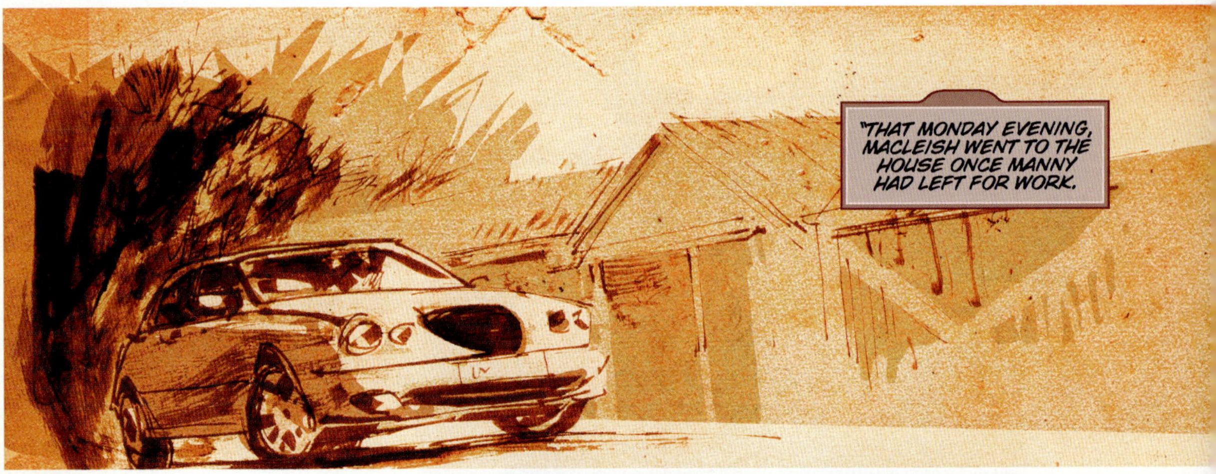
"THAT MONDAY EVENING, MACLEISH WENT TO THE HOUSE ONCE MANNY HAD LEFT FOR WORK.

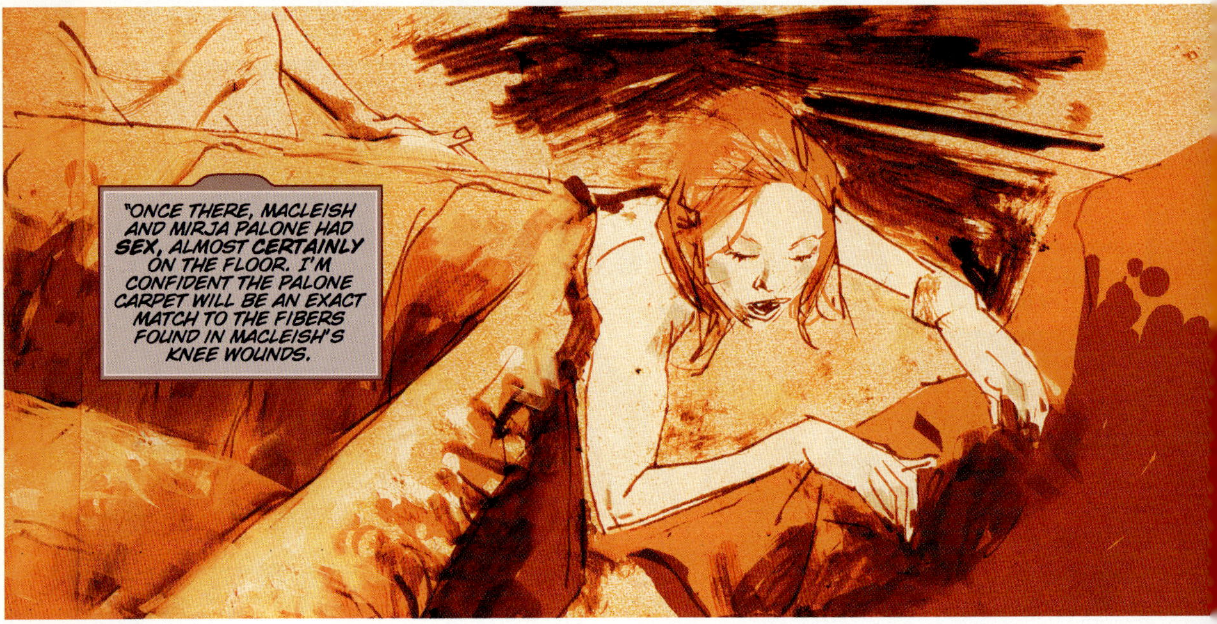
"ONCE THERE, MACLEISH AND MIRJA PALONE HAD SEX, ALMOST CERTAINLY ON THE FLOOR. I'M CONFIDENT THE PALONE CARPET WILL BE AN EXACT MATCH TO THE FIBERS FOUND IN MACLEISH'S KNEE WOUNDS.

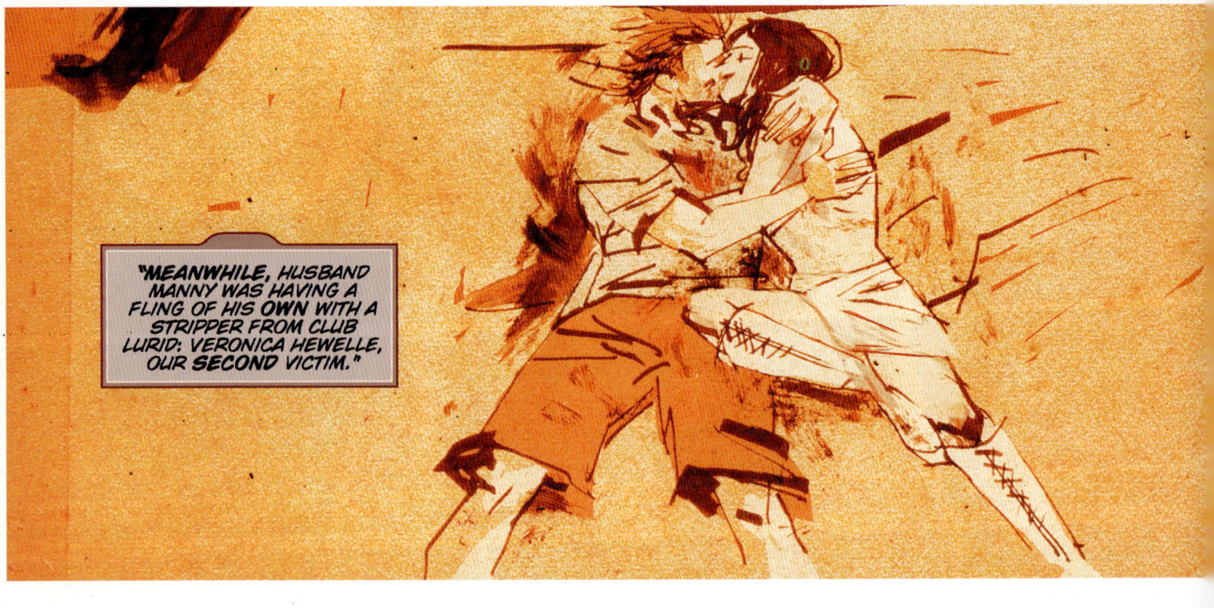
"MEANWHILE, HUSBAND MANNY WAS HAVING A FLING OF HIS OWN WITH A STRIPPER FROM CLUB LURID: VERONICA HEWELLE, OUR SECOND VICTIM."

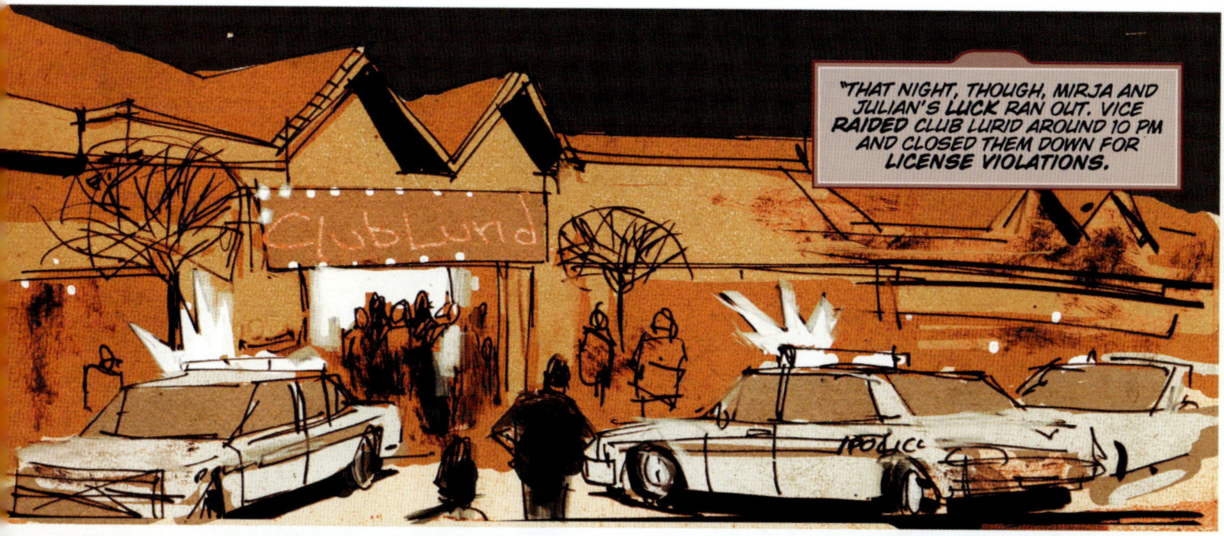
"THAT NIGHT, THOUGH, MIRJA AND JULIAN'S LUCK RAN OUT. VICE RAIDED CLUB LURID AROUND 10 PM AND CLOSED THEM DOWN FOR LICENSE VIOLATIONS.
ClubLurid
POLICE
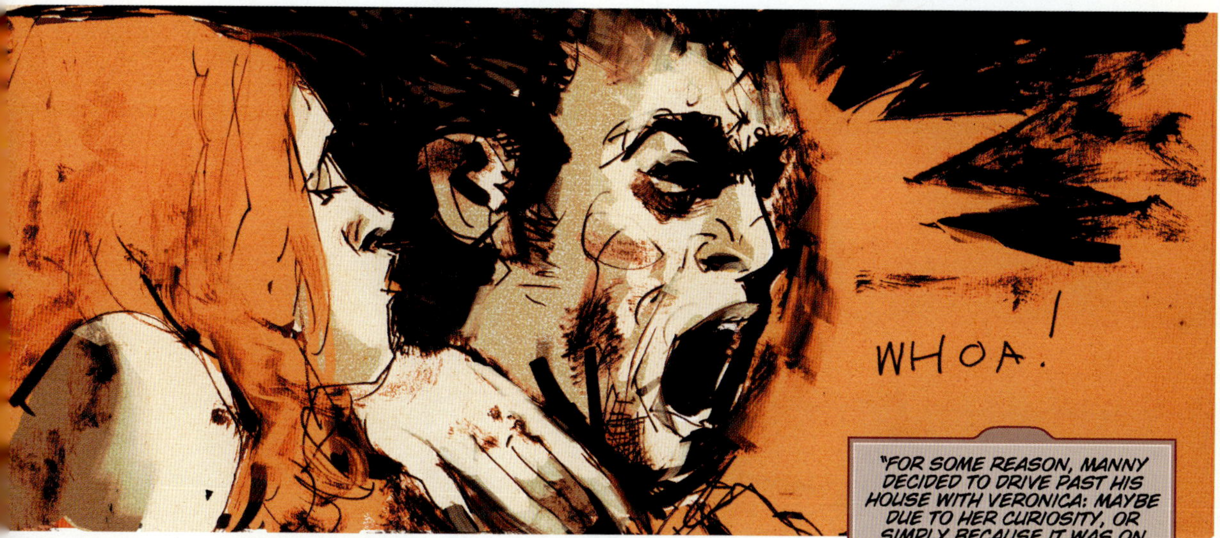
WHOA!
"FOR SOME REASON, MANNY DECIDED TO DRIVE PAST HIS HOUSE WITH VERONICA: MAYBE DUE TO HER CURIOSITY, OR SIMPLY BECAUSE IT WAS ON THE WAY TO SOMEWHERE ELSE.
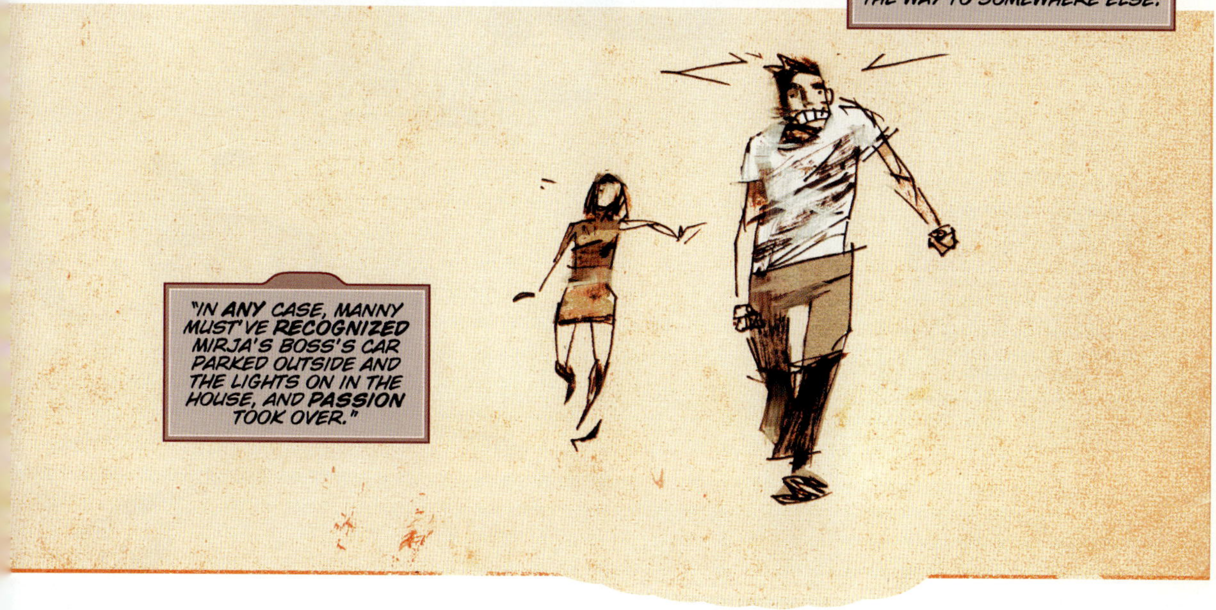
"IN ANY CASE, MANNY MUST'VE RECOGNIZED MIRJA'S BOSS'S CAR PARKED OUTSIDE AND THE LIGHTS ON IN THE HOUSE, AND PASSION TOOK OVER."

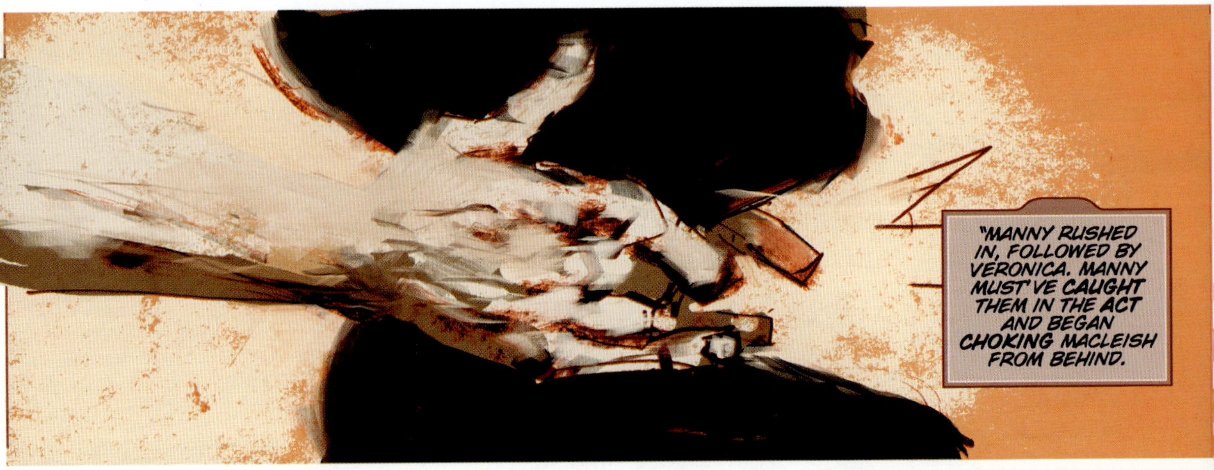
"MANNY RUSHED IN, FOLLOWED BY VERONICA. MANNY MUST'VE CAUGHT THEM IN THE ACT AND BEGAN CHOKING MACLEISH FROM BEHIND.

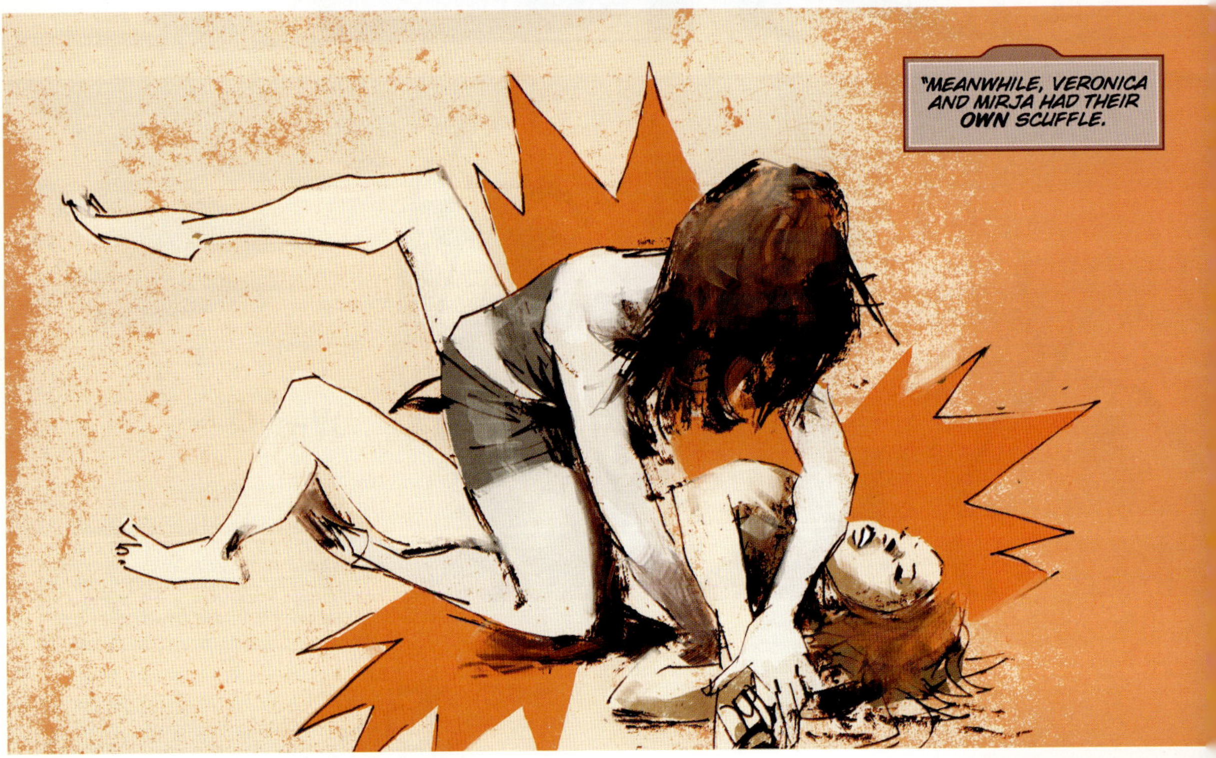
"MEANWHILE, VERONICA AND MIRJA HAD THEIR OWN SCUFFLE.

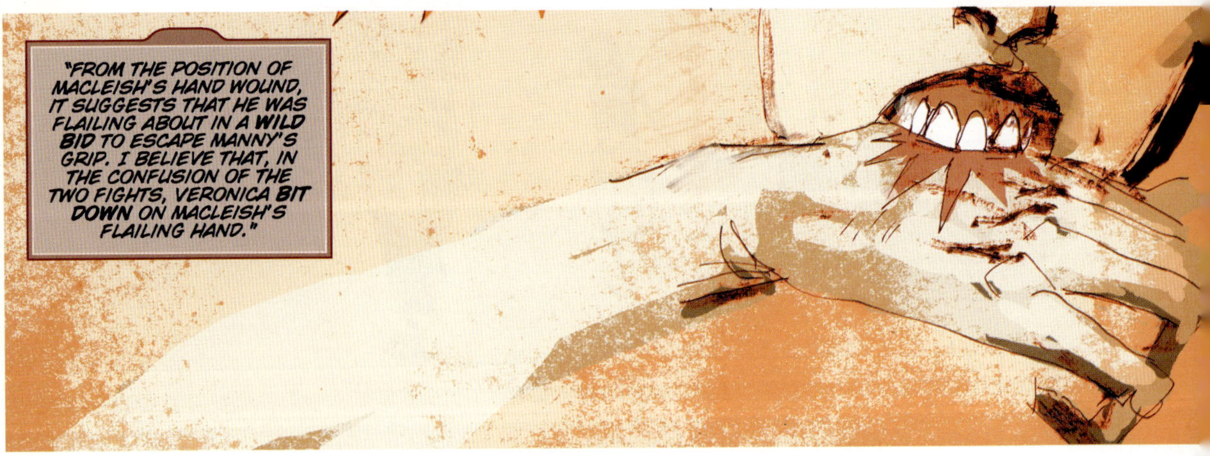
"FROM THE POSITION OF MACLEISH'S HAND WOUND, IT SUGGESTS THAT HE WAS FLAILING ABOUT IN A WILD BID TO ESCAPE MANNY'S GRIP. I BELIEVE THAT, IN THE CONFUSION OF THE TWO FIGHTS, VERONICA BIT DOWN ON MACLEISH'S FLAILING HAND."

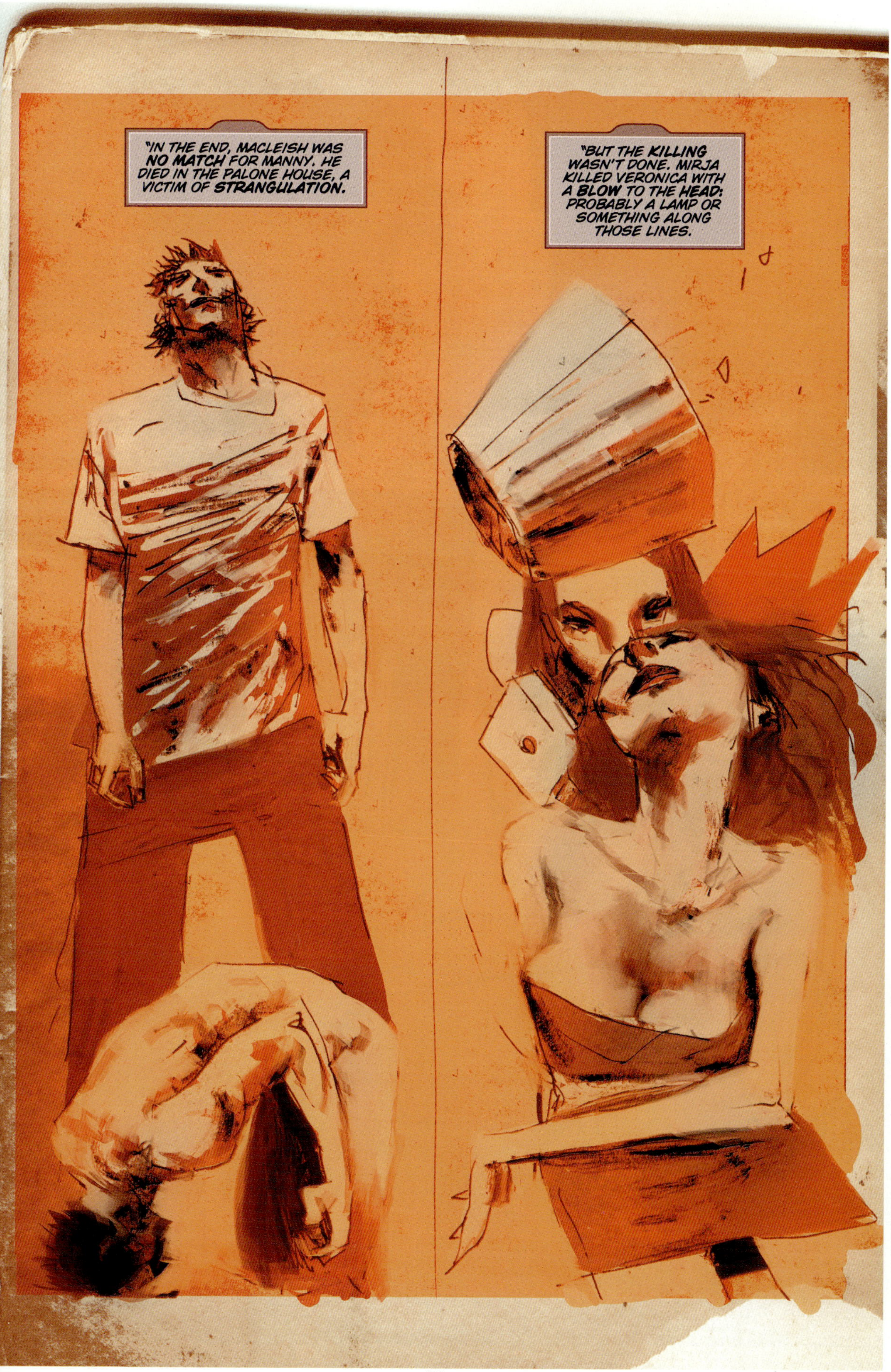
"IN THE END, MACLEISH WAS NO MATCH FOR MANNY. HE DIED IN THE PALONE HOUSE, A VICTIM OF STRANGULATION.
"BUT THE KILLING WASN'T DONE. MIRJA KILLED VERONICA WITH A BLOW TO THE HEAD: PROBABLY A LAMP OR SOMETHING ALONG THOSE LINES.

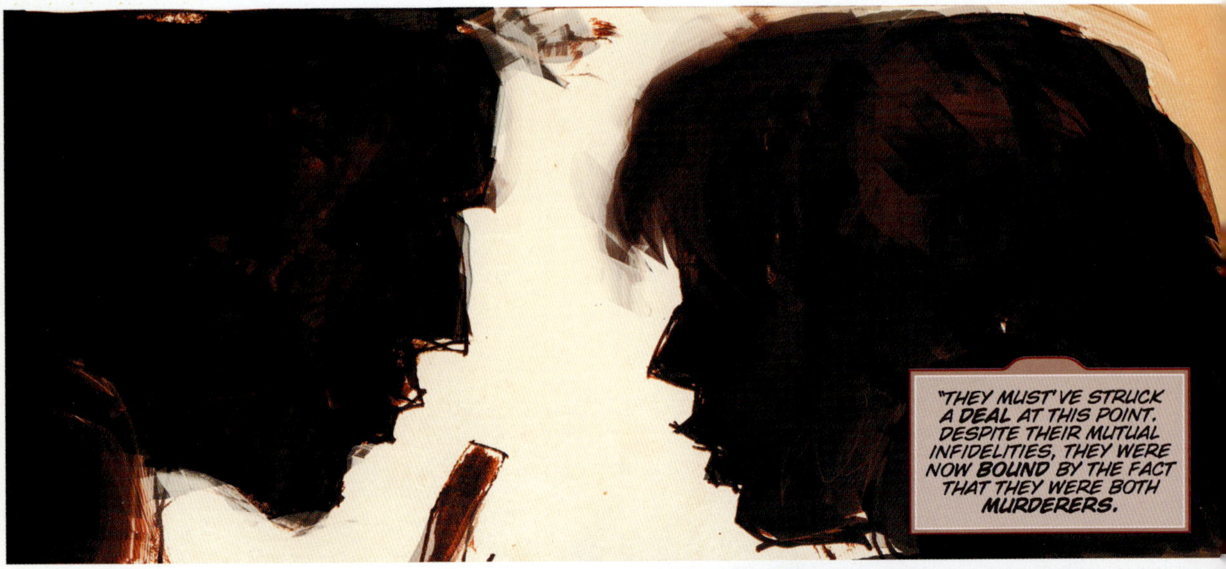
"THEY MUST'VE STRUCK A DEAL AT THIS POINT. DESPITE THEIR MUTUAL INFIDELITIES, THEY WERE NOW BOUND BY THE FACT THAT THEY WERE BOTH MURDERERS.

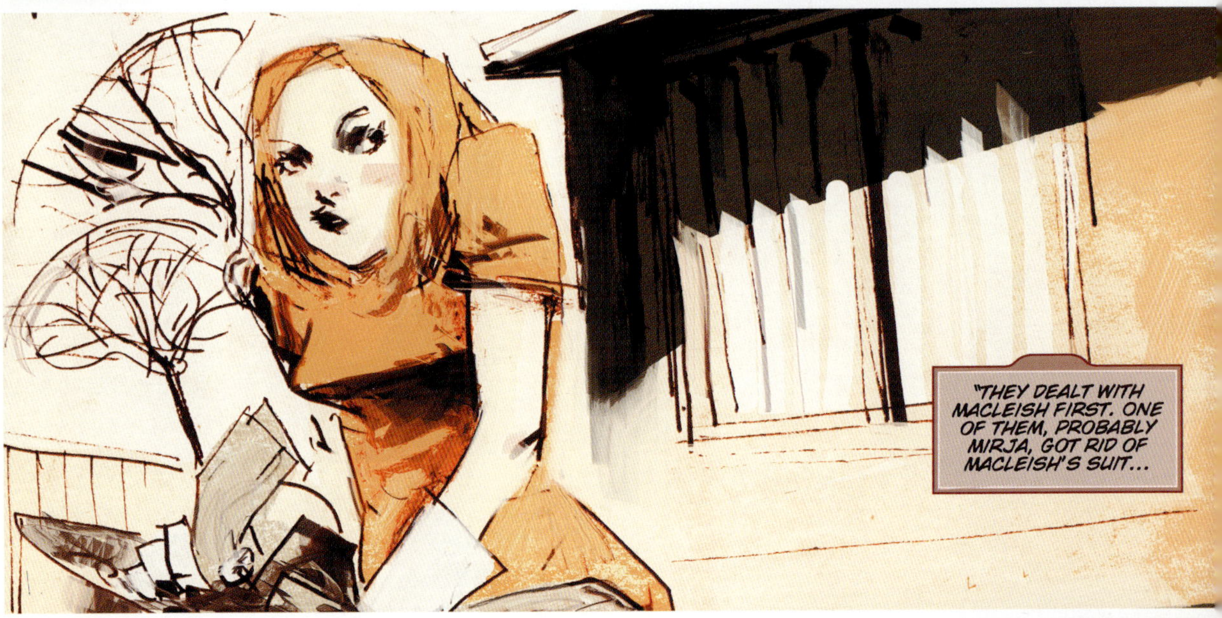
"THEY DEALT WITH MACLEISH FIRST. ONE OF THEM, PROBABLY MIRJA, GOT RID OF MACLEISH'S SUIT...

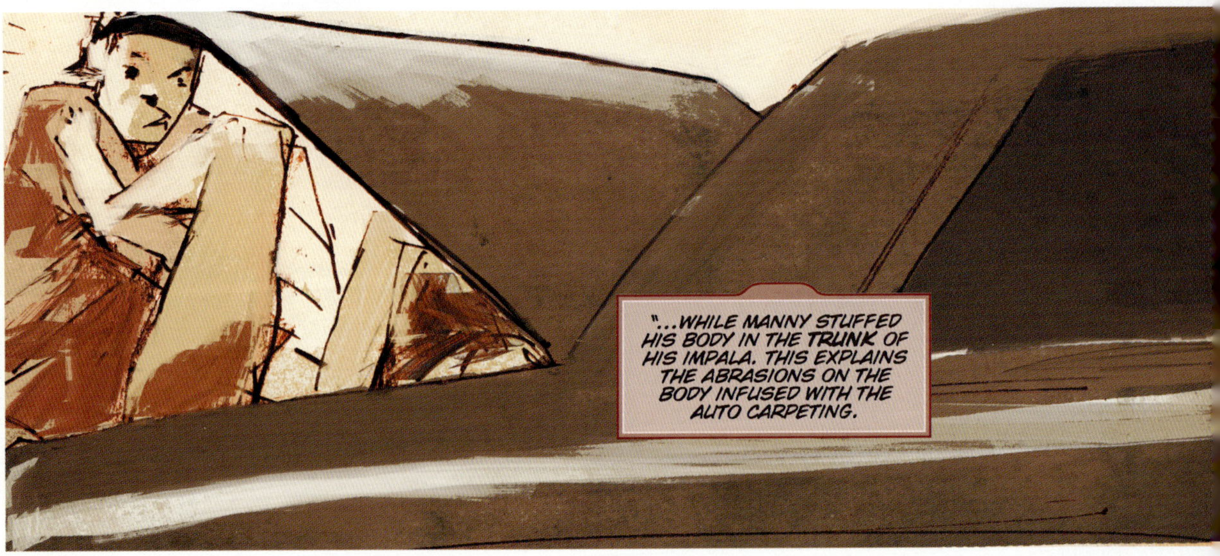
"...WHILE MANNY STUFFED HIS BODY IN THE TRUNK OF HIS IMPALA. THIS EXPLAINS THE ABRASIONS ON THE BODY INFUSED WITH THE AUTO CARPETING.

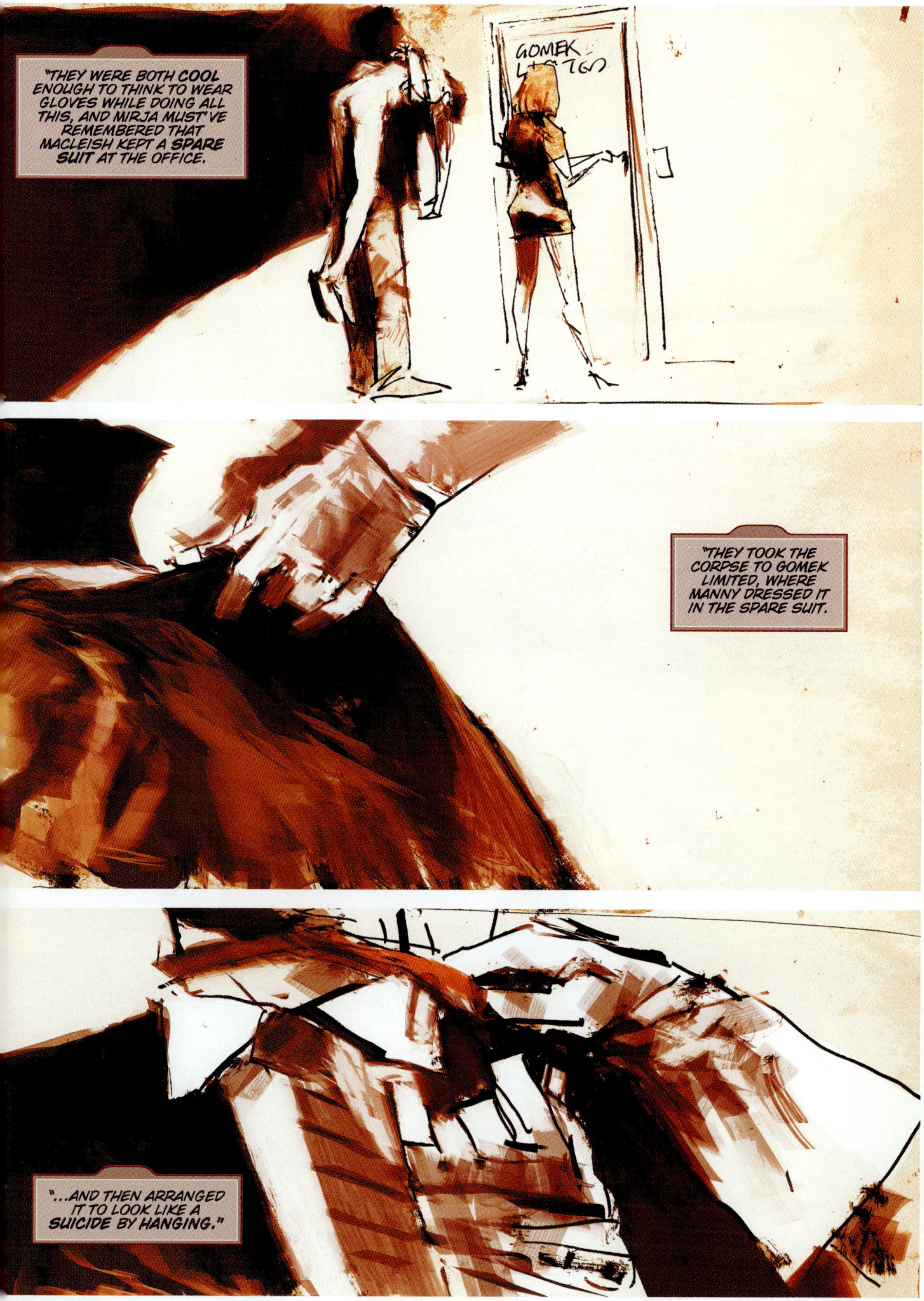
"THEY WERE BOTH COOL ENOUGH TO THINK TO WEAR GLOVES WHILE DOING ALL THIS, AND MIRJA MUST'VE REMEMBERED THAT MACLEISH KEPT A SPARE SUIT AT THE OFFICE.
GOMEK
"THEY TOOK THE CORPSE TO GOMEK LIMITED, WHERE MANNY DRESSED IT IN THE SPARE SUIT.
"...AND THEN ARRANGED IT TO LOOK LIKE A SUICIDE BY HANGING."

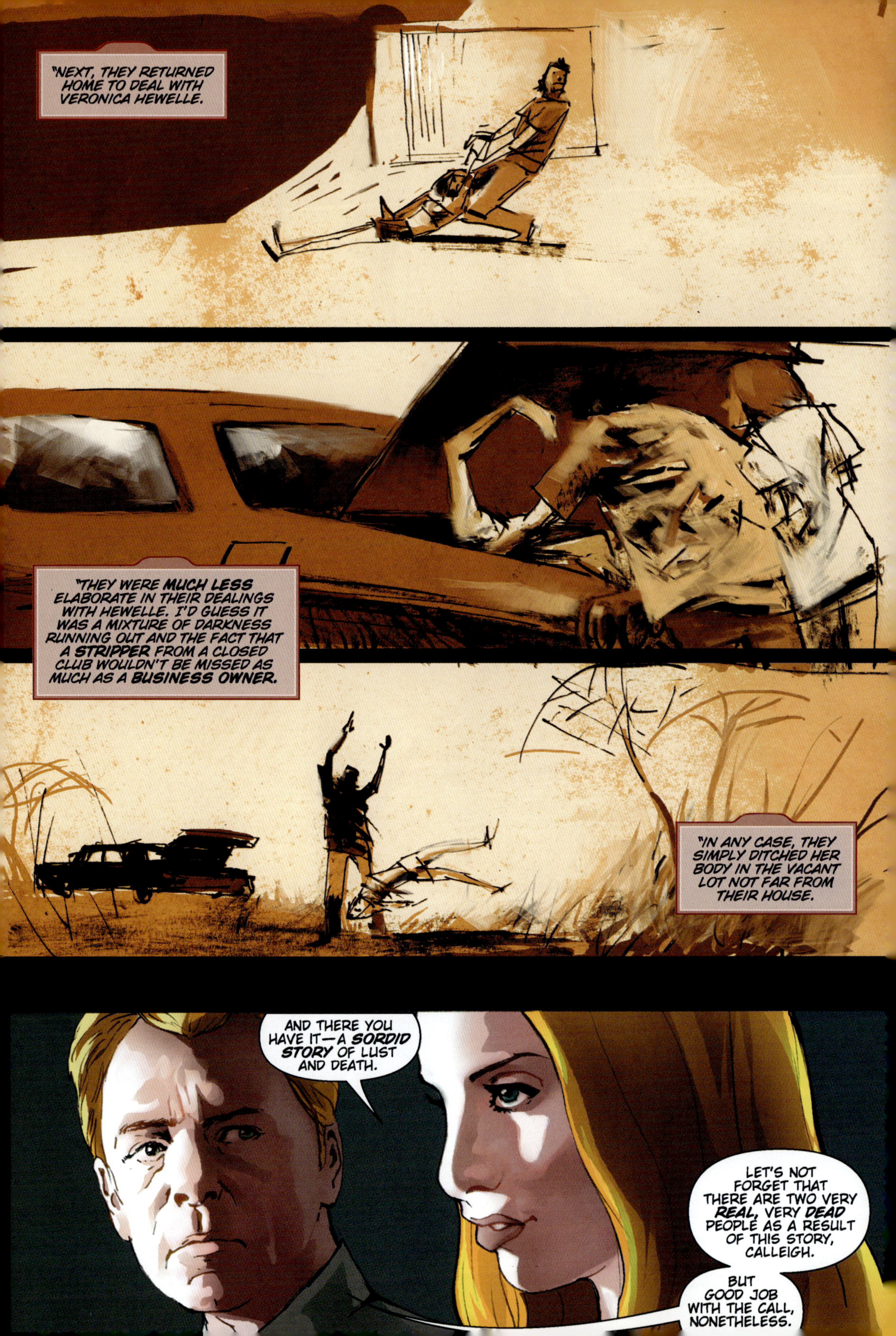
"NEXT, THEY RETURNED HOME TO DEAL WITH VERONICA HEWELLE.
"THEY WERE MUCH LESS ELABORATE IN THEIR DEALINGS WITH HEWELLE. I'D GUESS IT WAS A MIXTURE OF DARKNESS RUNNING OUT AND THE FACT THAT A STRIPPER FROM A CLOSED CLUB WOULDN'T BE MISSED AS MUCH AS A BUSINESS OWNER.
"IN ANY CASE, THEY SIMPLY DITCHED HER BODY IN THE VACANT LOT NOT FAR FROM THEIR HOUSE.
AND THERE YOU HAVE IT—A SORDID STORY OF LUST AND DEATH.
LET'S NOT FORGET THAT THERE ARE TWO VERY REAL, VERY DEAD PEOPLE AS A RESULT OF THIS STORY, CALLEIGH.
BUT GOOD JOB WITH THE CALL, NONETHELESS.

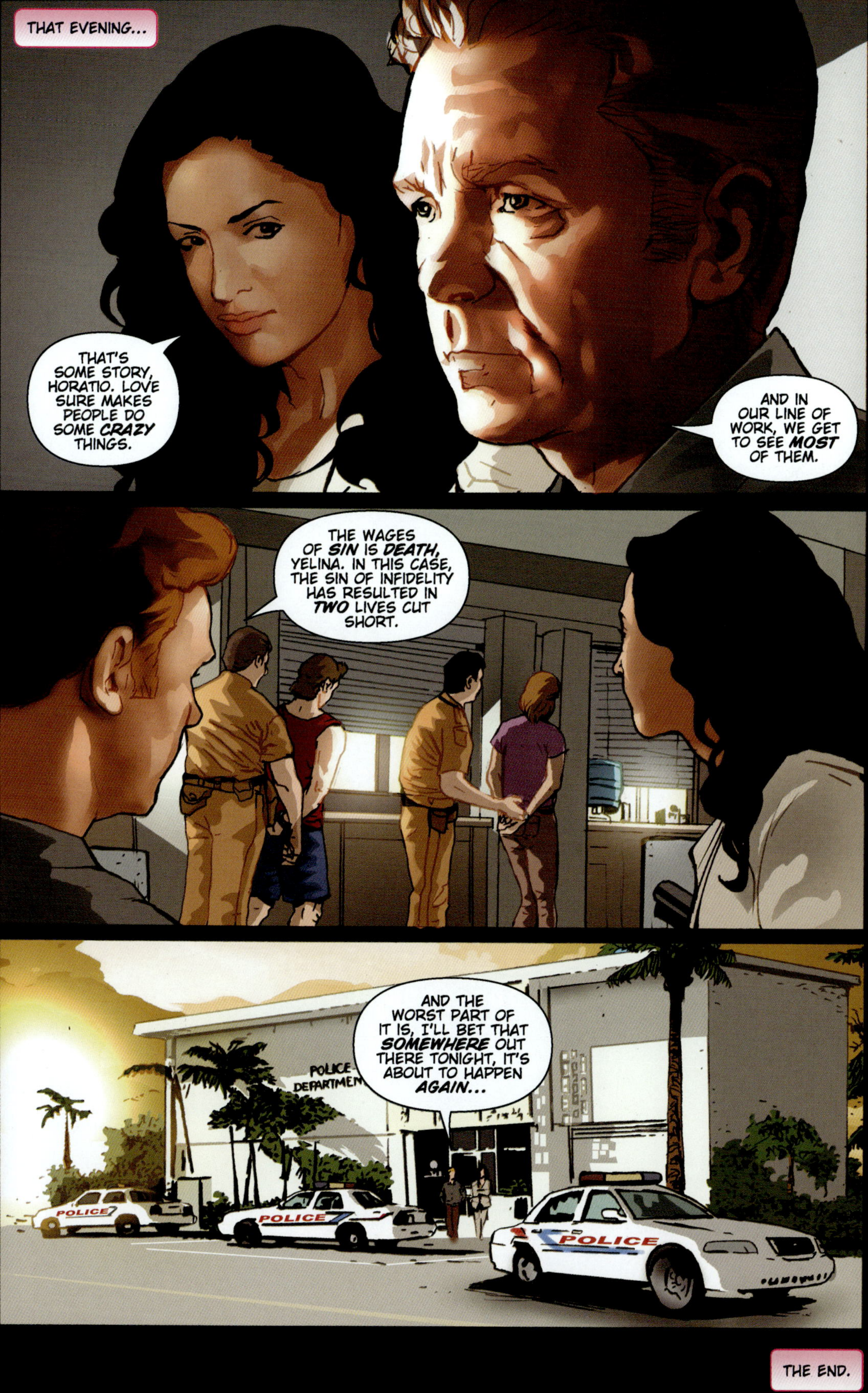
THAT EVENING...
THAT'S SOME STORY, HORATIO. LOVE SURE MAKES PEOPLE DO SOME CRAZY THINGS.
AND IN OUR LINE OF WORK, WE GET TO SEE MOST OF THEM.
THE WAGES OF SIN IS DEATH, YELINA. IN THIS CASE, THE SIN OF INFIDELITY HAS RESULTED IN TWO LIVES CUT SHORT.
AND THE WORST PART OF IT IS, I'LL BET THAT SOMEWHERE OUT THERE TONIGHT, IT'S ABOUT TO HAPPEN AGAIN...
POLICE DEPARTMEN
POLICE
POLICE
POLICE
THE END.

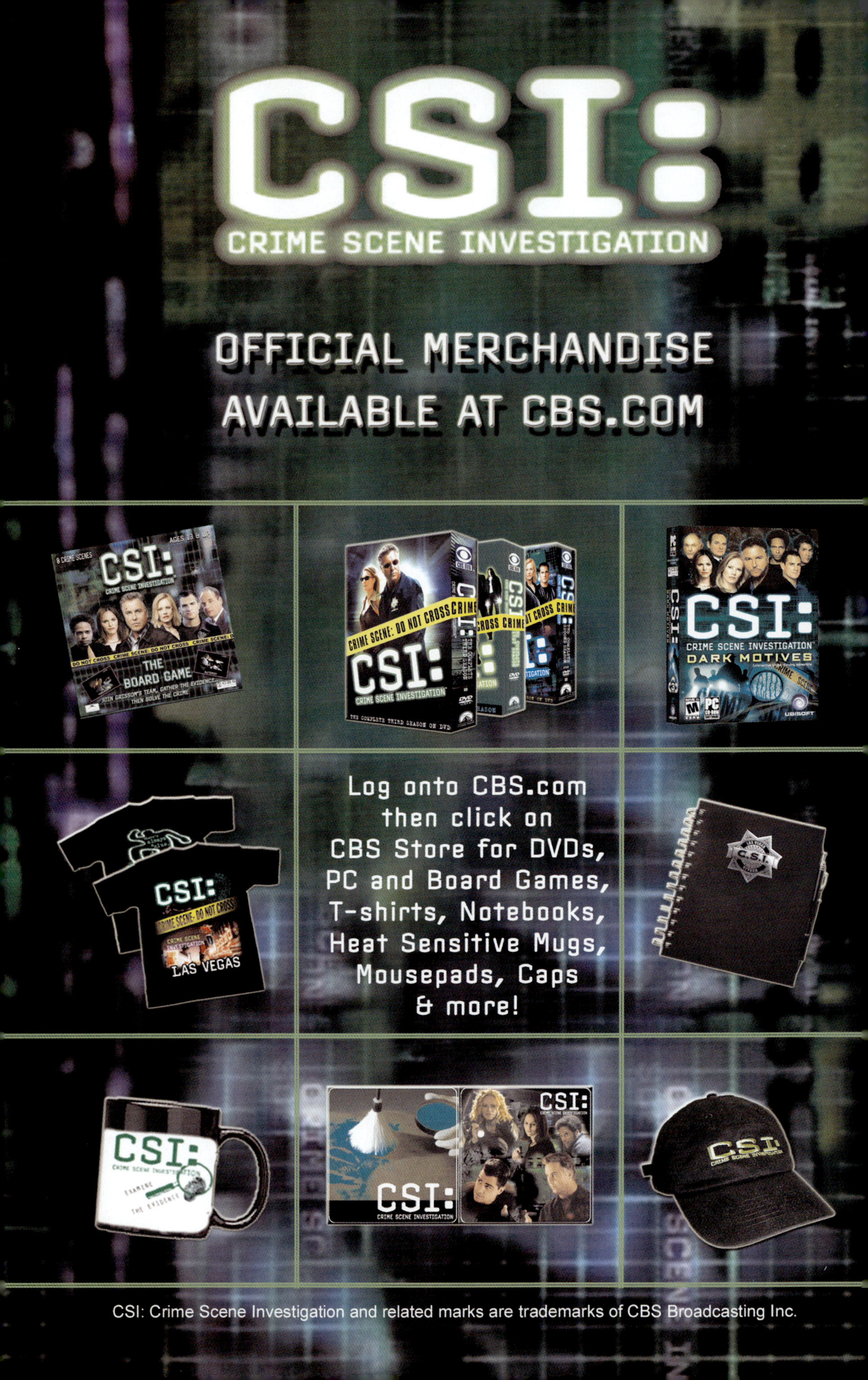
CSI:
CRIME SCENE INVESTIGATION
OFFICIAL MERCHANDISE
AVAILABLE AT CBS.COM
Log onto CBS.com
then click on
CBS Store for DVDs,
PC and Board Games,
T-shirts, Notebooks,
Heat Sensitive Mugs,
Mousepads, Caps
& more!
CSI: Crime Scene Investigation and related marks are trademarks of CBS Broadcasting Inc.

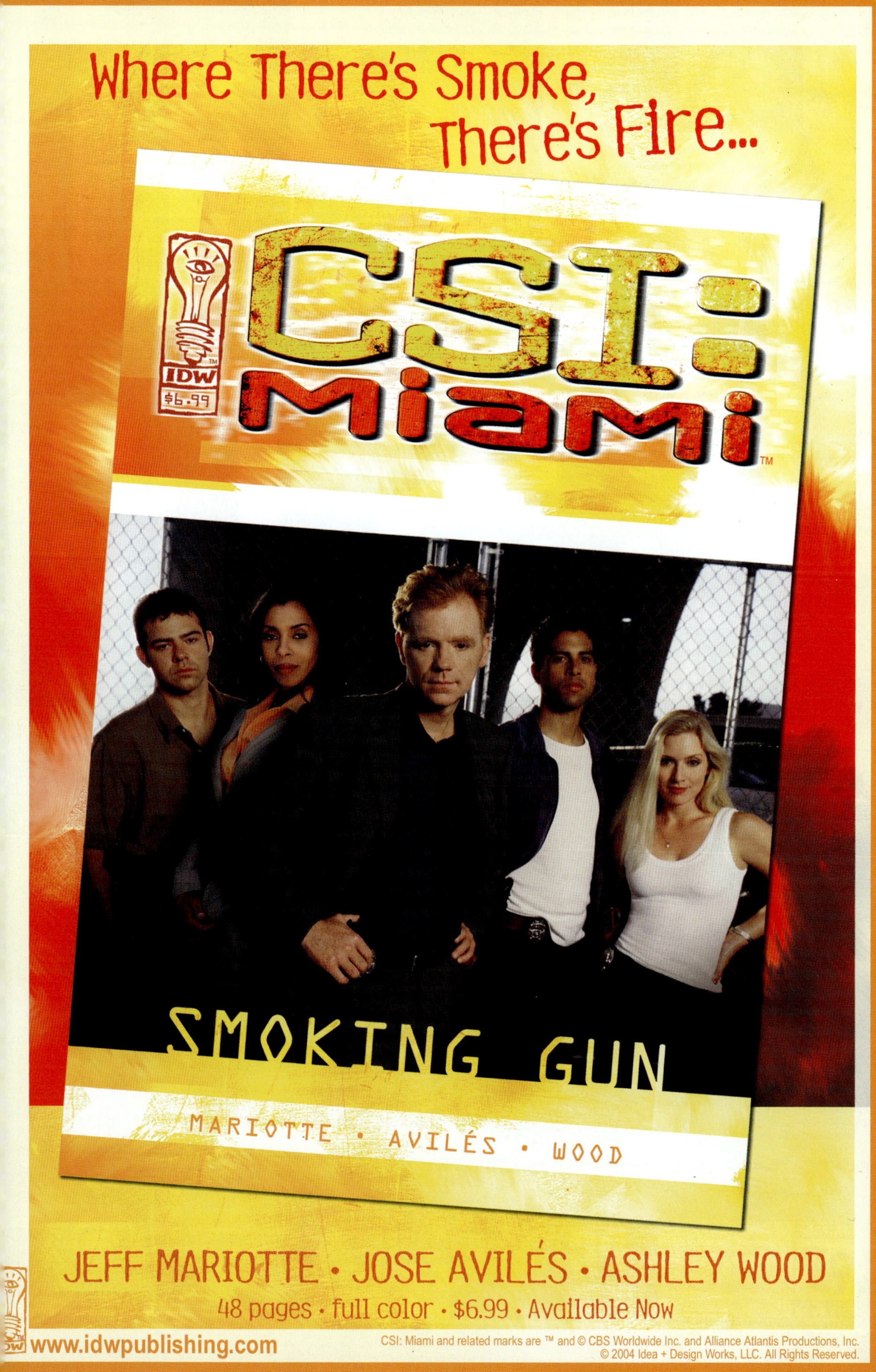
Where There's Smoke,
There's Fire...
IDW
$6.99
CSI:
Miami
SMOKING GUN
MARIOTTE • AVILÉS • WOOD
JEFF MARIOTTE • JOSE AVILÉS • ASHLEY WOOD
48 pages • full color • $6.99 • Available Now
www.idwpublishing.com
CSI: Miami and related marks are ™ and © CBS Worldwide Inc. and Alliance Atlantis Productions, Inc.
© 2004 Idea + Design Works, LLC. All Rights Reserved.

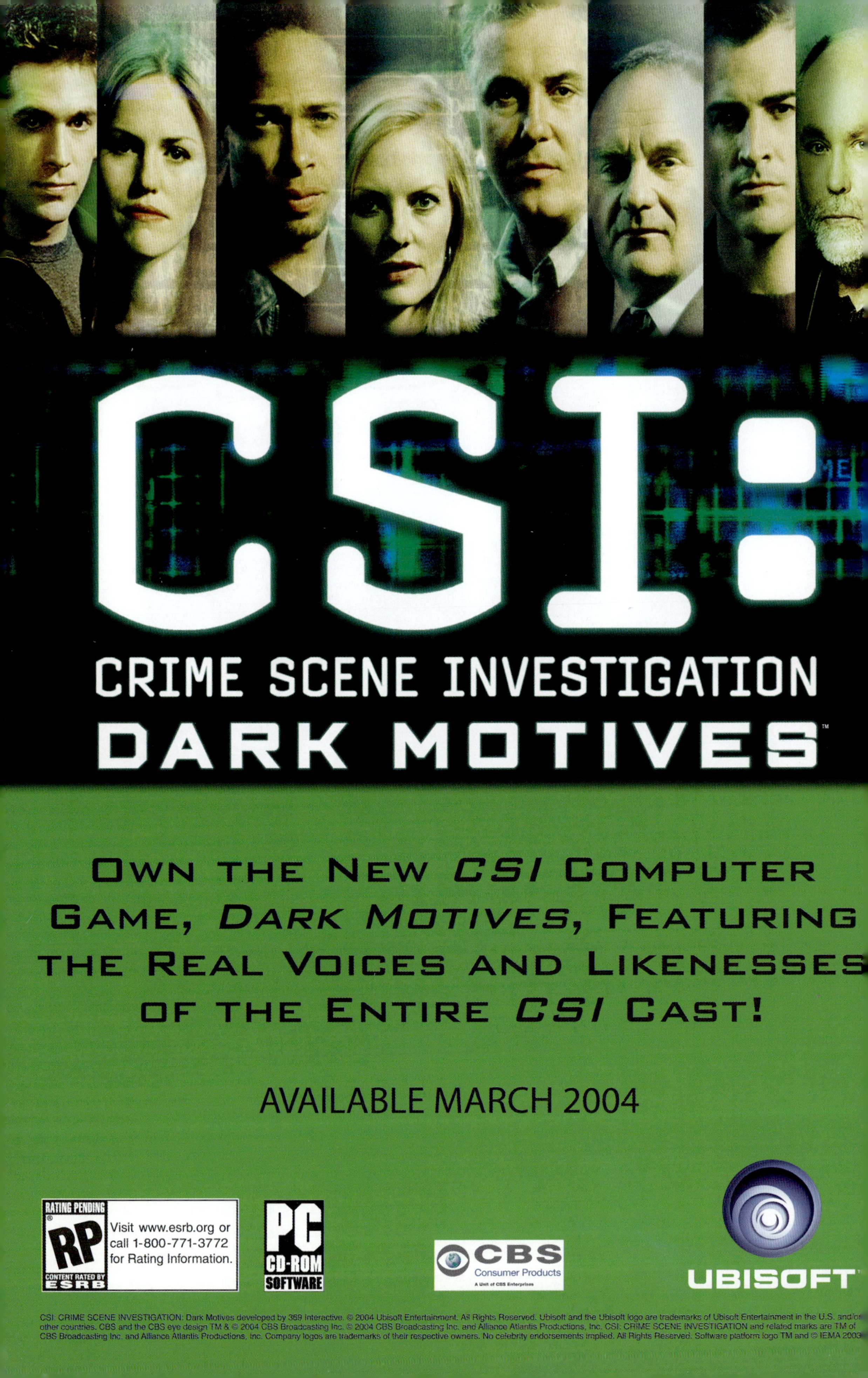